ILLUMINATE YOU

The Enlightenment Series, Book 1

C.M. Swan

CONTENTS

* * *

PART I

"What necessity is there to dwell on the Past, when the Present is so much surer—the Future so much brighter?" —Mr. Rochester

1. CATHERINE

S pacebar.
Enter.
Save.
Save.
Save.
Submit.

I'm staring at the screen, paralyzed at first, then a rush of emotions begins to hit me in waves. I'm going to lose it. No, I'm going to hyperventilate with this godforsaken mask on. I look up at my raised hand and then search around the room. My hand's in the air, right?! Where's the proctor?! I need to get out of here. Fast. Before I ruin this for 499 other future attorneys scattered around every nook and cranny of this arena. I look around the room again. Damnit, I can't seem to catch a proctor's eye. Wait, why am I the only one with a hand raised? I cannot be the only one finished. I look down at my analog watch. It can't only be 4pm. My brain just isn't reading the hands right. How did I just complete the North Carolina state bar exam with 45 minutes to spare and I can't read a fucking minute hand? Now I just feel like an idiot who totally missed something I should have caught! It felt good though. I felt confident. The essay answers just came to me and the sentences filled the screen like liquid ink through my fingers.

The sound of typing begins to take over my thoughts now. Fingernails and finger pads hitting keys. Typing. Incessant typing.

That's all I hear when the emotions begin to surface again. I've got to keep it together and get the hell out of here. I look up again and start to wave my arm about frantically. The blonde in the front finally sees me, looks at the computer to see my submission file waiting for her acceptance, looks at her watch and does a double take. I know honey, I feel the same way right now. Just quit second-guessing – I'm a freaking bar exam miracle, okay?! - and get the hell over here so I can bust out and finally start this quarter-life meltdown I've been putting off for this massive pain-in-the-ass exam. I bend over to zip my bag up, my new, over-the-top Prada dress suit choking me. God, I can't breathe in this thing and this damn mask is a reminder of serious, end-of-the-world shit I don't need right now. Mental Note: I am NEVER going into corporate law. I'd never survive the dress code. The proctor finally shows up at my desk when I'm about to stand up and pass out. She catches me before I stumble and checks me in, shooting me a concerned look before giving me leave to go. I look up one last time as I begin my run for the door and see Pierce glance up from his laptop. He looks at his watch before pinning me to the aisle with his eyes. I respond with a sad shrug as a lone teardrop slides down my cheek and my lips begin to tremble. "Go!" he mouths to me. I nod and bolt down the aisle and through the double doors as fast and gracelessly as my high-heeled feet will carry me.

The next thing I know I'm in my car. The car is moving. My body is making automatronic driving motions and I'm sobbing like a little girl. I've just lost my father. I've just lost my father in the middle of a pandemic. In the midst of completing law school and prepping for the bar exam. But the real kicker is that I've still yet to deal with the bigger life catastrophes of this past year – a shotgun wedding followed by a miscarriage, a failed marriage lasting all of three months and an ex-husband pushing the eject button on our sorry lives by signing up for active duty in Syria. And because someone must have decided we hadn't suffered enough, his first mission ended in bloodshed and mass chaos. Now he's MIA. My guilt is overwhelming. Our mistaken five minutes of bliss derailed him from his MBA and landed him in godforsaken Syria.

There are no leads on his whereabouts. Dead silence from his Commander. Silence from the White House. Silence from the Syrian Military. It's like he's dead. Sometimes I think I feel his death. But, no body has been found. We have one 20 second clip from the rebel force with hostages which we believe could be him and some of the men in his unit. Curt and I married 10 months ago, last summer. It was a rushed wedding. I was pregnant. Knocked up. He did the right thing by putting a ring on my finger but it wasn't the path either of us would have chosen. He went to college on an ROTC scholarship – first generation to attend college and smarter than anyone I knew. Perfect score on his SAT. Perfect score on his GMAT. Brilliant and so funny too. He lit up a room with his wit. One month later I miscarried. This forced us to face the truth we both knew from the instant the ring was on my finger – we didn't love each other.

I feel guilt for ruining his life. I feel broken and scarred. Sad. Drained. It took every ounce of energy to lift myself out of depression, to figuratively place a mask over my aching heart and bear down for months of bar-prep. And now this has all come crashing down. A wall of grief and I'm not sure I'm prepared to bear the weight of it. My Dad's death. The guilt I feel for not doing more to find Curt. The sense of failure I feel over the miscarriage and mistake of a marriage. The emptiness that has settled around me over the baby we lost. The lack of physical touch from this pandemic. I miss my Mom. I want to grieve with her.

I look up and find myself in my townhouse – what was once *our* townhouse – huddled in a ball against the front door. I have no memory of how I got there. My face feels stiff and puffy with streaks of dried tears. I look at my watch. 5 hours since I ran out of the exam. I search around for my phone and see a dozen missed calls and a bright shiny red circle with the number 20 on my message app. I'm lifeless. No energy to even pad my fingers over the touchscreen when the door begins to press against by back.

4

"Cat, are you there? Cat, is that you?" Pierce starts out by yelling and then dials his voice down as he becomes more aware of my pathetic ball-like presence in front of the door jamb. "Caaaat." He coos softly. "Baby, no. This won't do." He sings to me in a soothing voice. Baby?! Where'd that come from I think to myself as my mind begins to become more aware of how I ended up in this state. This is why people should never take on too many stressful life events in one year. *As if I selected them for myself.* Because a meltdown *is* inevitable. I was just waiting for it, wasn't I? My body begins to rise off the floor but without an ounce of help from my weak, exhausted muscles. Pierce carries me to bed and carefully lays me down, tucking me in under the covers. I can feel the whisper of his fingers across my face. Stroking my hair. Touch. Sweet touch. It feels so nice after so long. Not just the pandemic but after the baby and Curt. We couldn't find a connection. I wonder if it was ever there beyond a few mint juleps and one particularly amazing night when the sky felt bluer, the grass was an eye-popping green for miles and my body decided to develop fertility super powers.

My life is such a fuck-up I muse to myself as tears burst through again. I hear faint sobs. They're mine. Pierce re-enters the room with a glass of ice water and two blush-colored pills. I hadn't noticed he left the room in the first place. Why am I so out of it? Oh, yeah. I tried to be Super Woman for 6 long months in the middle of a global crisis and a personal life explosion. "Cat, you're exhausted. I knew this would happen. I told you to defer to the December exam. Baby, you need to take care of yourself. You've been through too much in one year. One person can't possibly handle one of these life crises let alone three." He preaches to me in his sweet, caring Pierce-voice. "Four. Five if you count the fact I just failed the bar exam" I manage to croak. God, I sound like Darth Vader. "Here take these and drink some water. You're dehydrated from all those tears, Baby." There's that word again. When did this start happening? As soon as I come-to, I've got to shut that down and fast.

Pierce Michael Buchanan III has become my rock and only saving grace through these three years of law school. He's the only reason I made it through the last nine months without a mental breakdown. Fourth generation Carolina undergrad. Third generation Carolina Law. He's a good kid. Loyal to his family. Tow the line and keep up the good family name kind of loyal. He does the right thing all the time for everyone and never once thinks of himself. He is Curt's best friend and saw us through the worst of this year. He's been by our side through the miscarriage and the fights, helped Curt through his decision to go active after we decided to end the marriage. He's been by my side since the day Curt went missing. I love him like a brother and he loves me like a sister. *Or so I thought.* It will always be that way for me. As I complete this thought, the back of his hand moves slowly across my cheek again while his other hand strokes down the back of my hair stopping at the base of my neck to grab my zipper. I turn to break the motion and the touch. It feels too intimate. Wrong.

He quickly backs away knowing he's crossed a line. "Cat, I'm so sorry, you need to get out of this dress though baby and get some rest." He whispers with a hint of huskiness that makes me stiffen. I turn toward him so it's not awkward and begin to speak in my kindest most feminine rasp "Thank you so much Pierce. I don't know what I'd do without y...". My words are stopped by the feel of the glass brought to my mouth. I swallow and realize how desperately thirsty I am and then proceed to down the entire glass in a very unladylike manner. "Advil?" he questions. I nod a rejection and he agrees to let it go. "I'm going to give you some privacy now baby so you can step out of this dress and sleep. I'll come by to check on you in the morning. And with a big hearty breakfast because I *know* you didn't eat dinner. And *you will* eat young lady. Even if I have to feed you with my own two hands. You understand me?" I nod affirmatively and smile making a mental note to shut down this baby shit tomorrow when I'm back to my senses. *If* I'm back to my senses.

I shed another tear as I feel Pierce's hand stroke my hair again and again; then I am lost to sleep.

2. CHARLES

"**S**adie, what the hell is going on? You know what kind of danger she could be in. Where the hell is security?" Why hasn't she responded to my text? It's been 15 hours since the arena let out. 15 hours since I texted her and it's still unread. Am I just an insignificant old acquaintance to her? She could be in danger. Shit, I can't handle this. I'm losing my composure. I knew I should have had Syd handle this one. Fuck the plan, I should have handled this one personally.

"Sir, apparently Security missed her departure from the arena yesterday and haven't been able to confirm she's in the house. Her car is parked outside though, Sir. I'm confident she's okay and that she's sa-"

"Sadie, how many times do I have to tell you, stop it with the Sirs, okay? Charles will do."

"I'm so sorry, S- I mean Mr. Draper. Old habits die hard. Twenty-five years assisting Dr. Mayvin, I just can't turn it off, Si..."

I breathe a long exhale. Keep it together Charles. This is what you do, the ultimate calmness amidst utter chaos, right? Of course, I would be the only one who manages to stupefy the world's most enlightened with my natural ability to *tune in* beyond anything they've ever seen and then proceed to lose it all at the first sign of a crisis. Is it a crisis or is it *her* that has me off balance? It's definitely *her*. Catherine Victoria Mayvin. A fucking goddess. *My* goddess. *Mine.* Christ, I can only hope. "No, it's okay Sadie." I mutter apologetically as I shake these thoughts away, "I'm the one who's sorry. I should never have raised my voice at you.

That was uncalled for. It's just been such a tense time and I'm having trouble *sigh* not being able to see to her safety directly given that she's not yet … enlightened *yes, that's the word* … to all that's going on."

"I know, Sir, and I think it's so sweet how much you deeply care for Catherine and all you've done to look after her father and the company. If she only knew, Sir. I wish you would let me or her mother tell h-"

"Sadie."

"I've done it again, haven't I, Sir?"

"Yes Sadie. Listen, just get Security on the line for me now please."

"Of course, Sir. But if it's any consolation, according to Security the car owned by their good friend Pierce appears to have driven off from the house earlier this morning so she must be okay, Sir."

Christ, this woman is getting on my last nerves. What is it with the good southern gentleman "friend" who gets to spend the night with her and not even Sadie "Mother Teresa" Jones bats an eyebrow? Fuck me. Friend. Yeah right. The man wants in her pants. If he touched her, I'll fucking kill him and fire the entire security team. Okay. Enough of this pining shit now, Draper. Get. Yourself. Together.

"Sadie, not a single word you just said made me feel an ounce more secured of her safety. Now. Get. Security. On. The. Phone. Okaaay?"

"Yes, of course, Sir. Hold for Security, Sir."

"Mr. Draper, I mean Charles, we have the building secured. Situation is under control."

"Thank you, Mr. ….?"

"Jamie, you can call me Jamie, Sir."

"Thank you, Jamie. I appreciate that the building is secured but have you confirmed the asset is safely inside."

"No Sir, I mean Charles, but we're confident she's in there. It's just that she must have left the exam earlier than expected and we must have missed her departure from the arena."

"Are you certain of this, Jamie? Would you bet your life on this assumption, because I did not pay for your security team to take chances and have your fucking heads up your asses. What were you doing during the six hours she was in that fucking exam, Jamie? Couldn't stand to sit in a fucking parking lot for six hours? Well, I'm not sure your twenty fucking thousand dollar a day services are worth a six-hour head-up-your-ass fuck-up to me."

"I'm sorry, Sir, it's just we weren't expecting-"

"Jamie, I don't want to hear another word out of you until it's affirmative evidence that she's alive in that townhouse. Do you understand me? Do you have any idea of what we're up against here? Clearly you don't. "

"Yes, sir. I mean yes I understand and I know this is an important job, Sir."

"I want a picture on my cell phone in the next 60 seconds or your entire team is fired! Got it?"

"But, Sir, you haven't authorized full surveillance services, Sir. I can't possibly get a photo without invading personal space, Sir. This wasn't authorized."

"Do it."

"Sir, I-"

"It's now authorized, Jamie. I'm hanging up now. You now have 45 seconds or this engagement is over."

Silence as I end the call. I swear to - Christ! Calm down, Draper. This is fucking insane. I've got to control my temper. What has come over me? The depth of this feeling. It's like no other and it's messing with my equilibrium and control. I've got to get back to the meditation room and find my balance again – it's the only way I'll handle this until she returns for the funeral. How's she going to take what I have to tell her? *How* am I going to tell her? Fuck.

My Samsung pings. It's a pic of my sweet girl from the front in her bedroom, her strawberry blond locks unruly but falling beautifully down the outline of her angelic face. Her eyes look sad. She's been crying I think. *Oh baby, if you would have just fucking waited for me, you'd be in my arms right now. I would take away all your pain.* And she's packing. Appears to be throwing a shirt into an opened rolling bag. Good girl. Come home baby, come home. *You're about to find out what's been going on in your life while you've been busy playing house and the good law student. Did you miss me? God, I fucking hope so. If I get my way, when I get my way, once I lay eyes on you you'll never leave my fucking sight ever again.*

Show's on Draper.

I pick up my Samsung. "Sadie, when does the Fall internship program begin?"

"Hello Mr. Draper. Not until after Labor Day this year, sir. Due to the pandemic we delayed the start. Why, sir? Is there a problem?"

"No problem. Connect me with Caroline please Sadie?"

"Caroline Benson, In House Counsel, Mayvin Enterpris... Oh, Charles. Hello. How can I help you?"

"Benson, I need you to push up the start date for one of your Fall legal interns. Got any issues with that?"

"Of course, Charles. No issues at all. Lord knows with all this vaccine press and Syria shit side-tracking us, we can use all the help we can get with the day-to-day." Who and when?"

"Pierce Buchanan and tomorrow, 8am start."

"Oh, pretty boy *the third*. Got it, Charles. Consider it done."

"Good." I say definitively and hang up. Pretty boy. Gotta love Benson! I couldn't have said it better. Pretty boy nuisance is now out of the way. Show's on Draper! And like an idiot, I check my text messages again. No new messages and my text to Catherine is still unread. As I scroll through my texts, I stop at her name headlining the text I last sent her "Catherine Mayvin". *My* Catherine. I love the way her name looks in print. The curves in the letters, the beauty and composition of the perfect combination of my favorite letters in the alphabet ordered just right to form her name, her beautiful name. Catherine. *My* Catherine. I read over my text to her again:

> Hey Catherine. Thinking of you today with your big exam. You're made of strong stuff, like your Dad. Leave it all in that arena. For him. Hope to see you this weekend. We need to catch up. C []

An ellipsis begins to animate in the reply bubble. There's my girl.

3. CATHERINE

I wake with a start. Rustling noises are coming from the kitchen. For some reason my thoughts jump to Curt missing in Syria, and I'm afraid, really afraid, for him and at who or what could be in my kitchen. Strange. I shake my head and it's like I'm clear again. Pierce is here. It's Pierce. Images of him putting me to bed last night begin to come back to me. The 'baby' shit. Oh yeah. I roll my eyes.

The smell of breakfast makes its way to my room – bacon mostly and hopefully eggs. God, I'm so hungry. And despite waking up a bit fuzzy, I am now starting to feel good. I feel great, actually. Starving, but great. Well rested. I peek at the clock across the room. It's 10am. I haven't slept this long in months. Who am I kidding! It's probably been over a year since I slept more than 6 hours. This is good. I needed this.

Wait, what day is it? The bar exam was yesterday. Check. Quarterlife crisis can now begin. Last night was its dramatic kickoff for sure. Check. Today is Thursday, July 30th. Shit, tomorrow's Friday. The funeral. Tomorrow's the funeral. Daddy! Oh, Daddy, I wish you were still here. I need to talk to you. You'd make it all better, have it all make sense. You'd fix me. Tears begin to form and I look up to wipe my eyes and catch the clock again. Shit! I've got to start packing. No time for breakdowns or tears. I mentally attempt the math – if it's 10am now that means I won't get out of here until... no way I'm missing rush hour traffic. I look down at the floor and see my new Prada dress, Louboutins and mask in a pile on the floor. Oh, we're in a pandemic. Traffic is a thing of the past. Good! Look out Northern Virginia, this basket-case of a life is coming home. For good *I hope.*

"Cat, are you awake?" And that's my queue to hop out of bed. "Yes, I am. Thanks for breakfast. I'll be out in a minute." I yell back to Pierce but can now hear he's on the phone. "Yes, Ma'am ... Absolutely ... Of course it's no issue ... I'm thrilled to be selected to start early ... Yes, Ma'am ... That won't be a problem at all ... You too ... Okay, and Ma'am?" He pauses. "Thank you so very much for this opportunity. You will not be disappointed."

By the time Pierce's phone conversation is over I know he must have been talking to Head Counsel at Mayvin Enterprises where he'll be interning this Fall. Mayvin is my Dad's company. Or *was* my Dad's company for 25 years anyway. Technically, I think it's now mine, mostly mine. I really don't know exactly. Shame on me, the good lawyer now, and I have no idea what legal arrangements have been bestowed upon me by my intelligent, ambitious, gracious, humble hardworking father. I've had my head in the sand about all of this Mayvin Enterprises corporate stuff since my life took a shocking turn last summer. How ungrateful of me. I believe majority shares are being held in trust for me until I'm 25. I mentally resolve to read the trust paperwork when all this settles down, after the funeral. My 25th birthday is right around the corner.

I throw on some running clothes from my hamper because it's the quickest thing I can find to throw on and join Pierce in the kitchen.

"Hey you!" He says, delighted to see me I can tell. So, I'm not baby today. Thank goodness! I was not in the mood for that awkward conversation. "Hi back at you!"

"You good this morning, Cat? You look good!" "Yes, I feel good. 12 hours of sleep did me wonders." "Cat, if you need to talk about anything, you know I'm here for you. Last night - Cat, you had a breakdown. You know that's what this is, right? You need to take things slow, okay? 12 hours of sleep is not going to cure this. These things take time, ba."

"Pierce, I know." I cut him off before he starts that shit again. "I've got this, okay? I'm strong. I've got Mayvin blood. Mayvin grit. And now I've got my Dad's spirit living around me. *I do, don't I?* I've got this. I really do. Thank you, Pierce. Really, thank you for everything."

"Of course." He says with a sigh. "I just wish I could drive back with you to Virginia. I worry about you driving and being alone with your thoughts. I was hoping to take you back myself, but I just got a call from Mayvin, I mean your company." He laughs. I roll my eyes. The last time I worked for Mayvin Enterprises, I was scrubbing toilets as a 16 year-old intern. Dad insisted I start with manual labor. '*No shortcuts for the owner's daughter*' he would say. Pierce continues. "And it appears I've been selected to start a month early. Apparently the legal department is crazy busy given the vaccine breakthrough and they need me to start first thing tomorrow."

"Vaccine?"

"Yeah, vaccine. He cocks his head and gives me a look of disbelief. "Cat Mayvin, please tell me you knew your company, the company you are to inherit, just hit a major breakthrough in the big race to develop a cure-all vaccine?" He mocks as if he's scolding a child. I reply guiltily "Pierce, you know I've done literally nothing for the last two months but bar prep, pack, watch every film adaptation of Jane Eyre ever made and run every mile of sidewalk and trail in this town to avoid a nervous breakdown. I know nothing about my Dad's company since I left for college. I don't even know the new CEO and shareholder everyone seems to think I'm so familiar with. Charles, my Mom calls him."

"Cat, it's all over the national news. Just look at your phone." "Oh" I whisper, dumbfounded.

"Okay, I'll give you this one. But, once we get you over these trying times, I recommend you accept the fact that you've got a pretty f'ing successful company on your hands and maybe learn a little about it. I guess there'll be plenty of time for that once you settle back in NoVa." He's so right. I owe it to my Dad to pay some attention to what he spent the last 25 years building and is about to be mine.

"Listen, I've gotta get on the road. Are you sure you're gonna to be okay driving on your own?"

"Yes, Pierce, I think at the ripe old age of 24 I've got the driving thing covered." I sass at him. When did he get so protective and fatherly? Pierce shoots me a hurt look.

"I'm sorry. I'm being mean and you've been nothing but a sweet-heart. Thank you for everything, Pierce. I mean it. Sincerely. I really don't know how I would have made it through this year without you." I manage to squeak out on the verge of tears. Again!

Pierce reaches out to pull me into a much-needed bear hug. "Shhh. Please don't cry. You helped me through this year too, Cat. Seriously. Listen, call me when you get in, okay?" I nod my head against his chest. "And I'll see you tomorrow at the fune ... oh no, actually, I won't. Cat, I'm so sorry but I think I have to miss your Dad's funeral. Unless ... I could call Mrs. Benson back and ...". I pull away and straighten my hair out of my face. "No! No Pierce, I'll be okay. I've got plenty of family and friends there to surround me. You don't have to be there. Go start your big legal career at my wildly successful company, okay. Seriously, I'm good."

"Okay, baby. Drive safe." He says as he quickly grabs my shoulders and leans in to kiss my forehead. Oh no! Not that again. I speak his name in my strictest no-nonsense tone as I pull away from him but he's running out the door waving good-bye before I can finish a sentence. Yeah, dude, you know you crossed a line. Seriously, what is up with him? Nevermind, I can't deal with this right now.

As far as I'm concerned love and relationships are not in the cards for me for a long, long time. Maybe never, honestly. After Curt and the baby, I'm so done with amorous complications. They just lead to hurt and pain.

The smell of bacon hits me again. Okay Cat, let's eat and get this show on the road! Honestly, I think I'm feeling a bit of excitement to finally be leaving this town behind. Too many painful memories. Maybe I really can start fresh back at home and maybe this chapter will finally end and I won't feel the need to relive it day after day. But then I think of Curt and where he could be right now and I again feel a tremendous wave of guilt. Who are you kidding, Cat? This will never be over. Not until Curt is found. If it weren't for the pregnancy, none of this would have happened and Curt would probably be home right now with his Mom back in Tennessee ready to start a successful post-MBA career. My disdainful thoughts are interrupted by a low buzzing sound. Shit. My phone. I haven't looked at it since yesterday morning before the exam. I flashback to last night and glancing at the number of missed calls and texts. Mom! Oh shit, she's probably so worried. I grab my plate and run into the bedroom to assess the damage. 5 missed calls from Mom. 3 missed calls from Pierce yesterday evening and a couple numbers I don't recognize. Mom first.

"Catherine honey, please tell me that's you." She blurts out after a half ring. "Yes, Mom, it's me. I'm so sorry. I should have called you right after the exam. I was just so exhausted. I came home and crashed." "Oh honey, I know. I heard all about it from Pierce." "Pierce called you. How did he know your number?" "Yes, honey he did and I really have no idea but honestly, honey, thank God he did. I was so worried about you. Such a sweet boy he is." Shit, Pierce called my Mom. He's really getting way too close for my comfort. I've got to distance myself from him for a while. He needs to take a hint – big time. "So how was the test?!" "Good, I think. Honestly Mom, it could go either way. I felt so confident in all my answers but then I finished way before anyone else so I really could have missed the mark somewhere." "I know, Pierce told me you left 45 minutes early. I'm sure it's fine. You studied so hard and you were so diligent to cover the material. I'm confident you passed honey." "What else did Pierce tell you?"

She proceeds to wax poetic about how sweet it was that he came to my rescue last night and that he was on his way to bring me breakfast this morning when he called. "Honestly honey, I think he likes you and more than a friend. I met him at your little quickie wedding and he's quite handsome you know." I'm disgusted at this conversation. "Mom, he's a friend. He's Curt's best friend for god's sake. Curt, my recently ex-husband, who has gone missing in Syria for the sake of world-wide democracy and freedom, Mom. How could you talk like that, Mom? Honestly, it's so disrespectful."

"Catherine Mayvin! That ex-husband of yours left on his own accord, on his own volition. He comes from a long line of military heroes. His own Mama told us Curt was itching to go active and be a hero himself. Don't you dare blame yourself for this situation. And don't you go there about the pregnancy. It takes two to tango, hon. He should have kept it in his pants if he didn't have a condom. I will not tolerate your insistence that any of this is your fault, Catherine. And don't you dare bring that attitude back here to Virginia! You understand me young lady? You're stronger than that. You're better than that. Besides, Charles has pulled out all the stops and Mayvin is doing all they can to locate Curt and the others on that mission. Rest assured, if those men are findable, Charles will find them. So, no more guilt. I can't take it, Catherine. Not with the funeral tomorrow. I need you in one, strong piece for me. Got it girl?"

How does she annoy me and make so much sense all at the same time? Only my Mom. "I understand Mom. I'm sorry. You've needed me these past few months and I promise to be truly present for you tomorrow. Present and strong."

"That's my baby girl. No apologies honey. Your Dad has not been your Dad for years. He's at peace now. This is the closure we've been praying for. I'm handling it surprisingly well, actually. *She really is and I suspect there are gentleman waiting in the wings already. Seriously, my Mom's a babe. The hot near-widow catch of Mclean, Virginia with a long line of suitors ready to swoop right in.* I think I've just had so much time to grieve the loss of him, you know?" I attempt to respond sympathetically but can't get a word in. "Cat, honey, I'm so proud of you and all you've accomplished this year in the face of some serious, honest-to-goodness adversity. Only children can feel so much pressure and guilt, I know from experience. Please, I don't want that for you. I'm good, really."

"Mom, 40 years was a long time to be married to Daddy. I'm sure you're not 100% good. I'm moving home Mom. We'll spend some much-needed time together. And we'll help each other heal. It will be welcome for me. I miss you."

"Oh honey, I miss you too. We'll talk about things when you're home. Okay?" I nod to myself but she doesn't wait for my reply and continues with her agenda. "Now, about your move. Okay, so Charles has arranged for Mayvin E's relocation firm to handle the entire thing – full service! Isn't that amazing?!" I roll my eyes. Why am I all of the sudden being handled like a VIP? *This is so not Daddy. Who is this Charles character, anyway? Probably some washed up former Raytheon mogul. This is googleable, Catherine. Well. He did manage to save the world in the span of the last two weeks, so I shouldn't be dissing him so quickly, should I?* I realize my Mom has been rambling while I'm alone with my Charles-bashing thoughts. "So, no need to pack anything and just pack a suitcase of your essentials for the next week and they'll have it all delivered to you back at the Mclean house in a few days."

"Mom, I've packed my entire house already."

"Oh honey, no you didn't. Really? I swear I told you not to worry about any of this especially with your exam this week. Oh well, what's done is done. And about the funeral tomorrow. So, Aunt Helen is taking care of all the details and Uncle Oscar is doing the eulogy. You and I don't need to be doing any of that. Neither one of us can make it through a hallmark commercial. So, no need to worry about anything. Your Dad gave them quite a parting gift apparently, so they have a sudden renewed passion for the legacy of their dear brother."

I giggle a little at her last comment. "Oh Mom, you always know how to make me laugh when I need it most. I love you, Mom." And I really begin to cry now.

"You see, this is exactly what I was talking about. Now, stop that crying nonsense right this minute, Catherine Mayvin. I have more news for you. So as you know, our dear friend Charles was so fond of your father, he has worked with all the leadership at Mayvin E and planned a celebration gala in his honor for this Saturday night."

Wait, what? Seriously? Who does this guy think he is?

"Really, Mom? This seems so over-the-top. Daddy wouldn't want this. He was so humble, so private. Also, we're in the middle of a pandemic. And why is this the first I'm hearing about it?!"

"Catherine, your father built something special and everyone who is anyone in the industry wants to honor him. It's such a coup. You and I will be guests of honor, Catherine. I'm told there will be a special tribute video Charles personally had produced to honor him. Please don't poo-poo this honey. It's important to me. Everything he accomplished before the dementia is being honored by the beltway royalty and frankly, Catherine, with all we sacrificed for all those years and now not having your Dad here by my side in our retirement, please don't take this from me or from him."

"Mom, I'm sorry. I didn't think of it like that. I was just ... no, you're absolutely right, Mom. I forget all you sacrificed to make that company work, for Dad's ideas and inventions to come to life. I'm just not really prepared to socialize beyond the funeral, Mom. It's so exhausting and I'm emotional and well, you know, having a breakdown here. But, I'll be there for you and for Dad."

"Oh good, honey, I'm so glad. The gala starts at 7pm Saturday night but Charles has all the arrangements made. Everyone in attendance will receive Mayvin's vaccination. We can discuss more when you get to the McLean house tonight. Charles has transportation ready to escort you to the gala and back. I believe he may have also arranged for a personal shopper so you should have an ensemble or two waiting for you to choose from at the house. *What the hell? What kind of over-the-top ... I hope they aren't charging the government for these frills.* I'll meet you at the house for dinner but I've almost entirely moved into the new condo on the waterfront which should give you some privacy. Honestly, honey, the house is yours as long as you need it."

"Mom, this is really all overwhelming but I'm so happy to be coming home at the same time. I need to go finish packing and get on the road. I *certainly* can't wait to see *our friend* Charles and thank him for all this ... attention. I mean, really!"

"Such a dear friend he's been to our family over the years. I can't wait for you two to reconne ..." Her doorbell rings in the background. "Cat, I've got to run, Uncle Oscar is at the door. Drive safe baby girl." And with that, she's off the phone. I'm sure with all the stress of the past few years, Mom is not remembering things correctly. I can't fathom in what context she thinks I've met this guy. I should look him up. I start to open the Google app but then I notice the 30 new text messages I've yet to read. I scan through and see messages from Pierce last night asking where and how I am – all OBE. Several more are from my study group chats all swapping notes on their exam answers. I DON'T want to look at these. Geez, these people are real masochists. Talk about living in despair for the next three months second guessing your answers on the biggest exam of your life. Delete, delete, delete, delete. Then I notice the yellow hearts bookending Charlie Hearst.

⬜Charlie Hearst⬜

Hey Catherine. Thinking of you today with your big exam. You're made of strong stuff, like your Dad. Leave it all in that arena. For him. Hope to see you this weekend. We need to catch up. C⬜

Wow, blast from the past. I haven't heard from Charlie since our annual text exchange on my birthday last fall (when I was in the midst of post-miscarriage depression and marriage turmoil). Of course, I feigned all was well and my life was perfect and he saw right through me. Charlie knows me all too well. He was my closest friend growing up. He and I were close, really close. There wasn't anything I couldn't tell him and that we didn't talk about and there really wasn't a moment we didn't spend together. Charlie came to our neighborhood to live with his Aunt Adeline the summer before our twelfth birthday and we instantly became friends. From then, we never spent a day apart until I left for college. Strange to think how close we were and yet we haven't seen each other once in the past seven years. He went to a local college in NoVa but then he dropped out and went to find himself traveling the world and ending up in Tibet (or maybe it was Nepal). He came back at some point and started interning with my Dad again – he and Daddy were super close. I think Dad became the father he never had and Charlie, with his inventive mind, reminded my Dad a lot of himself. I think Charlie still works at Mayvin. I wonder if he'll be at the funeral?

Memories of Charlie and me begin to flood back and I crack a smile. God, life seemed so easy and comfortable back then. I type a quick reply, throw my phone down on the bed and hop in the shower.

Hey yourself! If it isn't our international man of mystery, Mr. Charlie Hearst?! Back from Tibet so soon? Will I see you at the funeral? Would love to catch up! C ⬜ p.s. you stole my initial

The car is packed and I'm ready to leave my life behind in Chapel Hill. I run back into the townhouse for one last walkthrough before I get on the road and notice a black sedan slowly driving down the street, one I've seen out of the corner of my eye at least once before today. Strange. I thought this neighborhood was safe. Maybe someone's being watched by the FBI? Glad I'm leaving. Scanning through the rooms for the last time I'm stung by an uncomfortable feeling. I'm catching glimpses of sad memories that feel oddly like they belong to another. I linger at the doorway of one room in particular. The would-be nursery.

"You're even more adorable when you stare off into space like that, you know?" Curt embraces me from behind, nuzzling my neck with a sharp inhale. He can't get enough of my cheap coconut body wash. Curt's hands begin caressing my now visible baby bump and my head falls back, as I blissfully succumb to his adoration. "I'd be careful if I were you, Doe Eyes. The last time you had that dreamy look on your face, this happened." He chides me, tickling his fingers down my belly and sending goosebumps up my flesh. I giggle, landing further into his embrace. "The damage has already been done, so what's the harm in a little more fun?" Curt stills for a split second and before I can blink we're on the floor, limbs tangled.

I come back to earth after what seems like such a distant memory. That would be the last time we would talk to each other that way, we would touch each other that way. I miscarried the next day and with that loss, came the truth facing us both so clearly in the face. Something was calling us in another direction.

A melancholy feeling sets in as I drive away and it's only when I take the on-ramp to I-85 and settle into cruise control with a playlist of throwback songs that I begin to notice a fog is lifting in layers; the uncomfortable feeling begins to peel away and a carefree fun-loving girl I once knew, with the world at her fingertips, is showing her face again.

The blue ridge mountains begin to appear on the horizon and the vibrant green foothills stretch out for miles along the winding interstate. The sky is an electric blue scattered with eye-popping white, wispy clouds that appear to be painted in air by the hand of an artist. Their color contrasts and their vibrancy are breathtaking. I'm moved by this picture before me and it invokes such strong feelings with the music playing in my ears – Phish live – and I know I've felt this before and witnessed this intense beauty before. Then it comes to me and I gasp out loud.

Curt and I in the field, when we made love. It was my first time. We were making out. We'd walked off from the outdoor concert venue and could still hear the bands playing in the distance. The meadow was so beautiful. Curt was so insistent. He laid me down and we were close but before I could stop things I looked up and the sky was so indescribably breathtaking, vibrant and awe inspiring. I was overcome with emotion and passion. The feeling, like now, is like I could do anything, feel every molecule around me, see the essence and good in everything around me, love everything around me. I was so overcome and I kept staring into the sky and he was asking me a question, permission, and with each new touch of his mouth and hands on me I felt more intense. I managed to respond to his calling my name out in question, "Catherine? Answer me, please." "Yes", I whispered like a chant over and over. It was all I could manage to speak during the entire experience. Honestly, it was the most beautiful, moving experience of my life. Literally and figuratively orgasmic.

When it was over, it was like I woke from a trance. The sky didn't seem as bright and the field didn't appear as beautiful. I never had another experience like that again with Curt. Being in his arms after that never felt right like it did that night in the field. Thinking back on it now, it's almost poetic and so fitting that such an earth-shattering experience brought life into this world. I'm not surprised one bit and think, even if I had been on birth control, that sky was so intense, it might have made a deal with mother nature to have her way.

As I drive on and merge onto I-95 crossing into Virginia, it's like I'm following the vibrant sky the artist is painting out before me, leading the way. It's the strangest thing but the sky doesn't let up with this overwhelming beauty until I pull into the driveway of the McLean house. I don't remember the drive at all, it's like I'm in a trance again, like before in the meadow with Curt. I can't even manage to pull into the garage, I'm itching to get out and witness it for myself. I'm staring, dumbfounded, up into the sky in the middle of our circular drive when I hear my Mom open the door and call my name "Catherine, honey. You're finally home. Thank God. Stop gaping at the sky like a crazy person and get over here and give me a hug, honey." I reluctantly remove my head from the clouds and take a minute to remember where I am before I see my Mom and run to her. Once we're in our embrace, I never want to let go. Home at last.

When I finally open my eyes still rocking with my Mom in silence, I peer over her shoulder and see a black sedan race down the street in the direction of Charlie's Aunt's estate.

4. CHARLES

I'm in the meditation room. Who knows how long. Time doesn't exist when I hit deep. Hitting deep is not really something I've been able to articulate well, yet. Some refer to it as a unified mystical state yet this label lacks any meaningful explanation. I need to work on this for when the time comes with Catherine. When I'm deep, it's just me and the universe. Me, Catherine and the universe. I found her again. After the first time, I knew I'd always be able to locate her but the difficult part is that the draw and pull is so intense between us, it's an extreme challenge – a test of will and mental stamina - to not unite with her, to remain near without completing the act of being one spirit. I was so worked up with stress from the vaccine news, the Syria matter, locating Curt and Catherine's incompetent security team, it took me over an hour to reach this state.

I worry at times I may lose my abilities with my life choices especially entering back into the western world where there has never been another documented human to reach this level. When I hit the deep, it's like I've been traveling in an elevator to the depth of the earth, with pressure of gravity and all the earth's worries and woes driving me down, further. Then, abruptly, without warning, the elevator will stop and the pressure lifts. There's an overwhelming feeling of weightlessness and I'm floating. The first time I reached the deep, I described the trip to my guide and the elevator analogy with the sudden weightless feeling. His mouth went to the floor and he ran out of the house in silence. He returned with the elder guide who demanded I repeat my trip again as he bore witness. The elder knew from verbal legend I would reach enlightenment again quickly after the first time. He also knew the weightless feeling was not just spiritual and manifested, only in the most advanced cases, physically, through levitation. When I reached enlightenment – my unique version of enlightenment - before his eyes he witnessed my body rise, ever so slightly, from the dirt floor. I never believed this part, but he was adamant every time I would levitate higher, and that I was *"the most advanced case to have ever walked the earth"* (his words).

That second time changed my world, however, and hers too. As before, my spirit felt as if I had united with the elements around me and I became one with the soil, the sky, the trees, the universe itself. But my spirit immediately took on a mind of its own and I was suddenly there, with her, around her and then, *in* her; a feeling of incomprehensible completeness and love. I never wanted to leave.

When I reentered the present state, I saw the entire scene before me – where she was, who she was with and what had happened. I was overcome with utter horror, regret and anger. They carried me back to the elder's home but I refused to talk for days. I was filled with such rage, all I could do was run the mountain trails around the village and yell out in anger. Eventually, I was able to explain my experience. The elder knew what had happened to me before I managed to finish. That's when I became his understudy. I knew he was the only one who could help me control this and to never, ever make that mistake again. The elder turned out to be Yani, a revered spiritualist in Nepal who is said to have descended from a high nirvana spirit himself. The entire village, region and country of Nepal treats Yani like a god among men. Yani attempted, at first, to treat *me* as a god among men. I was the only high nirvana spirit to walk the earth in 250 years, after all. *Ironic name given my trips take me deep into the earth before my spirit can rise to be one with the universe.* But, I refused to accept his admiration. This precious *gift* of mine had harmed the one person I love the most on this earth and ruined the one hope and desire I have ever allowed myself.

I decided that day to devote my life to Catherine and her family and to do all I could in my power to right the wrong my selfish, adolescent desires had caused. Yani guided me in my spiritual journeys teaching me all he could from his family history; stories handed down from several generations before him. Most importantly, he taught me ways to temper my ever-present anger and rage from that day. He led me through intense physical training, mental games and challenges to sharpen my physical and spiritual self.

In Nepal, I was so physically and mentally sharp, free from western distractions, I could reach the nirvana state in under a minute. The process was so intense, it transformed me. Between daily trainings and evening trips to the deep, my body morphed into a broader, muscular frame. My teenage self would have killed to look like this. Yani explained to me that by continually reaching the highest (deepest) spiritual state, over and over, my mind and body were now out of balance. I had triggered my body to seek balance once again with my spirit. So, the morphing process began slowly until my frame became noticeably larger and broad only stopping when my physical and spiritual selves hit that balance of strength. The physical training helped my muscles grow and fill into my new body type and the mental sharpness helped me control my spirit during trips. I learned to seek her and be near her but I now have the power to resist our spirits' overwhelming urges to unite.

Here, in this world of distraction, it takes so much discipline and patience to achieve enlightenment. I am the anomaly, an enlightenment prodigy, and it takes me time in this side of the world with its focus on materialism and selfishness. It's no wonder our pandemic-ridden world is going to hell, a semi-enlightened state isn't even a possibility for most westerners. When I returned from Nepal to Aunt Adeline's estate home I had inherited, I knew

I needed an ideal environment to continue reaching enlightenment in my new life in the west. I came up with a plan to redesign the home with an elaborate deep, extended basement floor for a training gym and meditation chamber to enhance and stimulate the enlightenment process. I came up with a circular concept with one center cylindrical stone slab carved into concentric circular stairs that descend to the bottom onto a center meditation platform. I even set up cameras to record my trips to the deep and also confirm that I do levitate upon enlightenment, ever so slightly.

I've just arisen from the deep and I know Catherine is now home. I've led her here, or at least I know without a doubt my spirit followed her path along the highway until she arrived safely down the street. No doubt she saw my signature, but whether she truly felt my presence is another matter. In time, I can only hope.

I begin to climb out of the chamber when I hear the familiar sound of automatic bay doors rising from the secure annex. Her detail has arrived. Hope those jokers were discrete.

On the main floor, I find my phone and check it. A few urgent texts from Benson about Mayvin's statements to the Associated Press and tomorrow's epic day with the White House pandemic team. I'll reply to her later. She's a big girl making the big bucks with a team of outside advisors at her beck and call. She's got to learn to figure this out. I scan back over Catherine's reply and feel an instant pang of excitement, a familiar rush of emotion from my former self.

> Hey yourself! If it isn't our international man of mystery, Mr. Charlie Hearst?! Back from Tibet so soon? Will I see you at the funeral? Would love to catch up! C ▢ p.s. you stole my initial

I'm ready to fire off a reply and then stop myself. She still doesn't know. This is deceptive. Sort of. The sooner she understands everything, the better. This will be from Charlie, but it will be the last. That boy is gone.

Try Nepal, over 12 mos ago! Glad you're finally back home. Sorry, I can't be at the funeral. Vaccine has us slammed. I was here for him and your Mom when he passed. I'll see you at the memorial. We'll celebrate him then. But Catherine, if you need anything, just call me. I'm here for you.

p.s. you stole my heart

5. CATHERINE

Being home again is surreal. Knowing I'm here for good, single, law school behind me, no adult life to go back to, it's an out-of-body experience. I wander aimlessly around my childhood home trying to piece together memories growing up in these rooms and to feel a sense of place. It's difficult though. Mom has completely remodeled every surface in this house and the furniture is new, modern but rustic. Whites, ivories and khakis color each room with driftwood furnishings and metallic accents. As I walk through the space, it's therapeutic almost, as if I'm cleansing myself of the past and walking into a new, welcoming life. Wow, who knew interior decorating could be so life-altering. I like the way the space makes me feel. I can see myself rebuilding here. Bathing in the newness and cleansing away the marks of the past year.

And as if she's reading my thoughts, Mom's voice finds me from the open kitchen "It's cleansing, isn't it?" "That's exactly how I would describe it. Mom, you work miracles. I can hardly recognize the place." "This was my outlet. I would get so frustrated and depressed watching your Dad decline, his mind and body regressing so rapidly day after day. I threw myself into transitioning this space into what I wanted for him – perfection, peacefulness, beauty, cleansing, healing." "Well, you certainly achieved that goal, Mom, and I'm grateful for it too. This is exactly what I need right now, to put me in the frame of mind to heal and start fresh." "Oh Catherine, honey, I'm so glad you're home. You deserve so much more than what this year has brought you. I promise things will get better for you. Come, have a glass of wine with me."

Mom and I have nearly topped off the first bottle of sauvignon blanc when the Door Dash driver arrives with our dinner selections from Daddy's favorite Italian spot in downtown McLean. We've covered a lot of ground. The last month before Dad passed, her decision to bring him home full-time in his final weeks, sharing tears over the sentiments he managed to say to her in his rare moments of clarity, about Curt and the latest theories on his whereabouts from Mayvin and the Pentagon, bar prep, the exam and my sad, monotonous routine these last few months. Mom opens a bottle of red from one of the vineyards outside Charlottesville where she and Dad spent many weekends in the foothills of the blue ridge mountains.

Through dinner the conversation moves to the funeral and all the special details she's planned, the picture collages, the slideshow, the eulogy speakers, the virus precautions and what family we will and won't see in attendance and why. She moves on to the news of the vaccine breakthrough out of Mayvin's new biotech laboratory and how the press is overwhelming for the leadership. She explains that it's all-hands-on-deck coordinating production and distribution with pharmaceutical companies, FDA, CDC and the White House right now and it's impossible for anyone from Mayvin to attend tomorrow. Yet, Charles has assured her the special memorial event on Saturday will go on in honor of Dad, at all costs, no matter what.

I begin to wonder why this is only the first mention of Charles this evening. Over the past few months, it's been Charles-this and Charles-that during our phone conversations. I'm surprised she hasn't mentioned him before now. He seems to have been such a rock in her life, a saving grace to her personally, to Dad and the company, not to mention the entire country. And then it hits me. There must be something going on between them, a relationship perhaps, beyond friendship. I know my Mom too well. She wouldn't be talking about him so much if there wasn't something meaningful there. Well, if it's what I suspect, it should prove obvious on Saturday night. Oh Mom, I hope he's your next knight-in-shining-armor after what you've been through these past seven years. Figures, my Mom manages to find Mr. Right her first year in college and live 40 wonderful years with him and can't manage to be single for a hot minute before she lands another Mr. Perfect. Where did I go wrong?

The doorbell rings several times in a row and this time it startles me from my thoughts. "Oh, that must be the mobile med tech here with our vaccines. Charles told me to expect them tonight. He didn't want us being exposed unnecessarily tomorrow and everyone in attendance on Saturday is required to have a vaccine administered by Mayvin no later than tomorrow evening – 24 hours before the event." As my Mom hurries to the door I continue my train of thought. This Charles guy is 100% smitten. That's exactly what it is. How dense of me not to see it until now. I check myself on this development. Am I upset? After all, my Dad did pass away only 3 months ago. Why does the prospect of my Mom seeing another man not bother me? I just got a divorce after only a few months of marriage – barely even had a marriage – and it doesn't feel right for *me* to be thinking about anyone in that way. I think it's because my parents had something so special, so perfect, they were true soulmates and life partners, I know nothing would or could ever replace that. My Dad would want my Mom to be happy without her.

"Catherine, are you coming? They're ready for you now. We're in the front hall." Our vaccines are administered in no time and as soon as the med tech shuts the door my Mom is practically rushing behind them. She can't seem to get out of the house fast enough. I quickly wonder whether she and Mr. C are already shacking up. Geez Mom, could we bury Dad first? Perhaps I'm jumping to conclusions. I should really give her the benefit of the doubt. She's probably just tired and has two epic days ahead of her greeting and chatting with friends, family and beltway big-wigs. That woman's got to get to bed. There's a flurry of activity in the kitchen and I see the lights from a car pulling up in the driveway. Is that a driver? I sigh. This is so not Dad. What would he think of all this?

"That's me, honey. I've got to go get some rest." "Are you sure Mom? Can't you just stay here tonight?" "Oh no, honey, I haven't been able to sleep in this house since your Dad passed. Too many memories for me here, even with the new décor." Oh, that bad huh? Poor Mom. Her feelings must be so complicated right now. But who's driving her, anyway?

"Is this driver service safe, though? Do you need me to follow you?" She laughs out loud and then stops herself. "Oh, I'm sorry honey, you don't know everything yet but it's not my place to ex-plain. I have a driver service and a security detail all wrapped up in one. As do you. This Syria thing is more complicated than just Curt, honey. Charles will explain everything after we get through the services. I don't think he wanted to trouble you with the weight of it all. Don't worry about anything though. We're safe and in good hands with Charles's crew. I promise you."

What. The. Fuck. I'm trying to make sense of every bit of non-sense that just came out of her mouth and also trying not to yell at her. If there's anything I can't stand it's being kept in the dark like a child, especially about things that involve me directly. Fucking security detail? When was she going to tell me this?

"Mom, what the hell? I can't believe we sat here for three hours talking and none of this came up. You can't just leave now! Spill, Mom. I need *way* more details than this. What the hell do you or I need security for? How can we be connected to *anything* going on with Curt and Syria? You must have misunderstood something Charles told you, Mom. Seriously, this does not make sense at all?!"

My Mom is visibly flustered. I've upset her I can tell. She's struggling with how to handle my reaction, but I'm not letting down. Seriously, what the hell? This is a really alarming thing to just casually mention on the way out the f'ing door.

"You're right, Catherine. You're absolutely right. I should have said something earlier. You know, I probably have my story mixed up on what the security is needed for. Maybe it's the vaccine publicity. This all just started a few weeks ago. I didn't want to bother you with anything I heard from Charles given you were in the midst of exam prep. Please don't be upset. I'll make Charles tell you everything on Saturday before the memorial, okay? Will that help?"

"Mom, I appreciate you trying to protect me but I'm not a headcase, you can and should tell me anything Mom, especially if it involves me and my life and *most* especially if it involves our safety! What do you mean it's not your place to tell me?!" My voice is raised now and I'm being theatrical. I've had too much wine and I need to take this down a notch. What will this accomplish but getting her upset and me more upset. She doesn't know anything more. I'll save my angst and rants for this Charles character and get some digs in about him stepping in on my Dad while I'm at it.

"Please, honey." She pleads with me "Please just wait until Saturday, okay? I promise you the house is secure and you're in good hands and I'm in good hands. Just wait to hear the whole story from Charles on Saturday. I promise it will all make sense, then. Please understand why I didn't share this with you. I need to go now, okay?"

"Mom, go to the condo and get some rest. I'm not upset with you. This is just all really surprising to hear and there have been a lot of changes going on here with the house and the company and I'm just feeling really in the dark about what has happened with Curt and this Charles just seems like an enigma to me."

"I'm so sorry you're feeling that way, honey, and you're right, there's a lot more you need to know about the company and I'm just so glad you're finally home. Tomorrow, funeral. Saturday, memorial. Let's just get through tomorrow and take this one day at a time, okay?"

We're standing at the front door now and I open it for her, leading her down the front steps. "Goodnight Mom. Get some rest, okay? Love you". It's beginning to drizzle and the driver is standing out in front, waiting with the car door open. She blows me a kiss and waves as she heads to the car. Strange new lifestyle I've come home to. Security details and drivers. What the fuck is going on that would require a full security detail for our family and what does it have to do with Curt? I shut the door and lock it behind me. Maybe my Mom is mixing up stories. She's had a lot going on the last few months. It could just be the vaccine publicity. I decide to drop it and get myself in a better state of mind. The next two days are going to be challenging enough. I don't need to be jumping to conclusions. I try to put myself in my Mom's shoes. I never would have told me about this either if I were her. Okay Mom, you win. Issue dropped. Charles better spill the beans on Saturday though. But then a thought occurs to me. The black town car I saw in North Carolina before I left, the same one I saw speed down the street when I arrived home. Was that my security detail? Had they been watching me in North Carolina? My blood starts to boil. I'm suddenly furious. Bury it, Catherine. Bury it for now. I resolve to bury it but if this Charles character turns out to be a Grade A asshole, I will fire his ass on my 25th birthday and not think twice about it. How dare he keep me in the dark about something like this? Who the fuck does he think he is anyway?

I march back into the main room after locking the front door and fueling my own anger along the way but am suddenly struck by the sound of Sinatra serenading me in the background. I remember my parents used to dance, actually more like hug each other closely and sway along on the hardwood to Sinatra songs. I know what my mom means about not being able to sleep in this house now knowing he's gone. Poor Mom. I hope I wasn't too hard on her. I really should go straight to bed but I'm still too rattled by the "security detail" news to sleep.

I attempt to connect the house speaker system to my Spotify account which takes me about 20 minutes longer to figure out than it should - this is the kind of tech idiocy I bargained for when I settled on law school - and pour myself another glass of wine. I scroll through my phone and see texts from Pierce, my law school friend, Vicky, who's going to work for the ACLU in Atlanta, Curt's Mom, Melinda, and Charlie. I reply to Vicky first and ignore Pierce. He needs a reality check on the nature of our relationship.

Vicky's a sweetheart to check in on me when she's got enough life on her hands with the move back to Atlanta as a single Mom. I could talk to Vicky about everything I couldn't share with Pierce. She always made me laugh when I needed it and inspired me to finish law school when I just wanted to quit and move back home. If Vicky could do it with the cards she was dealt in life, so could I. Melinda, Curt's Mom, was just checking in to let me know she'd be at the funeral tomorrow. Melinda and I are really close. I've thought about going to stay with her in Tennessee for a while, until Curt is found – dead or alive. She's like a second Mom to me and she gets me. She wasn't upset about our divorce or the marriage even. She has life figured out and just takes it as it comes. She's enlightened. I don't know many people like that, honestly. She has a healing quality about her and she's got this Curt missing thing under control too. Such confidence that "what will be, will be" so no sense in getting all upset about it. I'm in awe of her. I reply back and send her a heart emoji. No sooner do I hit send and I'm getting an animated goodnight kiss and hearts in her reply. She's such a sweetheart. Seriously, not a bad ex-mother-in-law. Not bad at all.

I read Charlie's text. Another validation that this vaccine development has Mayvin in a swirl. I know Charlie was at my Dad's side the week he died and he's not even going to the funeral. Geez. I have a lot to catch up on with Mayvin E, as my Mom calls it. I decide not to reply to Charlie either. I'll see him Saturday.

A Beatles song I was obsessed with in high school begins to play and my thoughts linger on Charlie. I wonder if he's still at his Aunt's house down the street? What happened to his cousin, Aria? Where'd she go to school? Has she graduated? I wonder what he's like now? What does he do at Mayvin? *Mental note to ask Mom tomorrow.* I wonder if he's seeing anyone? Maybe he's married. No, I would have been invited. Would I have, though? I got married and didn't invite him. But then again, I didn't invite anyone really, other than my Mom. Dad was too sick to attend and in no mental state to comprehend it.

I'm unpacking my suitcase in my old bedroom that, aside from the antique four poster bed in the center of the room, looks nothing like my old bedroom. The bathroom is souped-up and dreamy with an oversized claw-footed soaking tub and a walk-in, glass-walled shower with a gazillion sprayers. *Thank you,* Mom! The walls are painted a pale sage green color that looks more grey in certain light and decorated with a fresh white painted wainscoting you'd find in an old sea cottage in Maine. My bed is stuffed with a mountain of throw pillows each with a hint of sage green in its pattern to tie in the walls and the duvet is overstuffed and inviting. I want to fall into it and never come out. The dark mahogany poster doesn't go with the modern décor in the rest of the house but I know my Mom could never part with the only reminder she has from her childhood home in Western Pennsylvania.

I'm reminded of one of the last times I laid in this bed. It was with Charlie. We knew our lives were about to change and we'd not see each other again for months (little did we know it would turn out to be years). We were sad but anxious for the new chapters ahead. *So* over high school. We had always been friends but things were changing between us. The imminence of our parting brought us closer. We used to hang out in the main room or my basement or in his Aunt's overgrown backyard that abutted the CIA building fence line. I usually made him listen to my favorite lines from the Brontë novels I was so obsessed with, mostly quotes from Jane Eyre. He was so tolerant and so intelligent too. He would always say something insightful that made me see the lines from their books in a new light. Anyway, there was something about those last weeks together that made things more intimate between us. We still acted like friends but we would each look for excuses to touch each other. His hair always fell in his face and I would sweep it back. He would do the same with mine and sometimes we'd sit for the better part of an hour just listening to music and touching each other's hair or face or hands.

Then, one day, 3 days before I left for UNC undergrad, I was lying on my back in this same bed and he was laying on his side facing me, his head propped up on his hand. He began to touch my hair and stroke my face. We both turned to each other and stared for a solid minute – forever it seemed to me – and I finally leaned into him and we kissed. A long, slow kiss and when we finally broke it I was flush and hot all over. I think he could tell. His gaze moved to my chest and his hand began to follow. I don't know why, but I knew what he wanted and I wanted it too. I'd never been touched before. I'd only ever been kissed by a boy, once in middle school and again early in high school, but no one I liked enough to take it any further. Charlie began to change for me in that moment and I could see him as more than a friend. I was surprised at how suddenly the feeling came over me. All of the sudden, it became clear how much I trusted him and loved him for the friend that he was to me. I knew I wanted to show him how much I felt for him and I was dying for him to touch me.

He began to lift my shirt up to where my bra began. I couldn't wait for him to take it off. I only broke my gaze from him long enough to lift my shirt off entirely and unhook my bra. I even unbuttoned my shorts for him and he slid them down to my ankles. Charlie began slowly caressing my body with his hands from my shoulders to my chest to my breasts, my nipples, my stomach.

His hands worshipped my entire upper body until he reached my pantyline. All the while his gaze was glued on me. My breasts, my stomach, my mound, my legs. It was the most erotic experience I had ever had. My panties were drenched. I was on fire and about to burst. I reached out to begin touching him too. I could tell he was aroused. He called my name and said softly "Catherine. Catherine, I ..." but we were interrupted by my phone ringing on the night stand. I was so startled. I didn't want to stop but the phone kept ringing and I couldn't ignore it.

When I answered it, it was my Mom. That was my Dad's first episode. He was at work and couldn't remember where he was or what he was doing there. She was scared and needed my help. I was panicked. Charlie helped me get dressed and drove me to the office. The next three days were a whirlwind of doctor's appointments for my Dad and preparing to leave for school. Charlie and I never had time to talk about what happened or deal with what we were feeling for each other. That was seven years ago. I rack my brain for news I've heard about Charlie since and to whether he is seeing someone or married. I register a pang of jealousy at the thought. I hope not. What a lucky woman she would be.

6. CATHERINE

My new driver, Tom, drops me at home alone after one of the hardest days of my life. It's around four in the afternoon and I'm spent. I've shed tears and been in different stages of mourning over the loss of my Dad for the better part of a year, ever since the dementia took over. But the finality of it all today, the casket and the burial. It was too much. I have no more tears to shed. No more words to say. Mom was amazing. I was in awe of her. Her composure. She always knew the right thing to say to each family member or friend or colleague. She even sat with Curt's Mom and me for nearly an hour catching Melinda up on the latest news Mayvin and the Pentagon have learned on Curt's case, which was virtually nothing. I think about all she's done for Dad through the years and, today, was the grand finale. I attempted to hang with her and I'm exhausted, beyond the pale. My head hits the pillow and I'm instantly out – my new Prada suit dress and all.

Curt's pacing in front of me as his hands glide over the minutes-old buzz cut. "But this is so sudden! Geez, Curt, we can make this work. Just give it some time!" I try talking sense into him. "Cat, I'm a Starnes. This is what we do. It's in my blood. Something's calling me, okay? I don't know how to explain it." He stops pacing and turns to me. "Look at me Cat. Just please look at me." He pleads. Arms folded, I stare unbelievingly into his eyes. "I'm not running away from you, okay? I love you. I will always love you. Nothing will change that. I'm giving you a chance to start over because I love you. And, I need to see this through. For me, okay?" He's made his way across the room and his arms are on my shoulders now, moving with his words, attempting to convince me.

"This needs to be a divorce, okay? A clean cut. I will be gone too long. What I need to see through for myself, it won't be quick, Cat. This will be a journey. And, when I come back, if our lives cross paths again - if some man has not swept you off your feet - I can only hope we'll have another chance at happiness. But, in the meantime, Cat, I won't make you wait for me. I would never be that selfish." He's searching my eyes, looking for me to understand. I can't speak. This is just too much to comprehend. I want to make this easier for him but I'm too hurt. My baser instincts prevail. "Selfish? Leaving me right now is selfish, Curt. Divorcing me within weeks of a miscarriage is selfish. Why did you even get married if you had "this feeling", "this urge" to join the Army, Curt? Why even bother marrying me? You ruined my life!"

Curt lets go of my arms, hurt registering in his eyes. "Please don't say that, Cat. Please, please don't." Tears begin to form and my face flushes with hurt and sadness. He turns away. "I can't stand to see you cry, Cat. This is breaking me. I need to go. You'll see in time, this is for the best. For you especially, Cat. I've taken care of everything. The money is all yours. There's an attorney handling everything and he has explicit instructions - anything you want or need is yours, okay? I won't be reachable for a few weeks. Melinda knows everything. Please talk to her. She will be the shoulder I can't give you right now."

I wake with a startle. Something has me unsettled. I listen for a sound but there's only silence. The main room, maybe? I'm suddenly really frightened and my mind turns to Curt, lost somewhere in Syria. I recall waking up with this same feeling the day after the bar exam. No doubt today's events including my conversation with Melinda have my mind reeling. Painful memories can be unsettling. What time is it? The shades are drawn. Is it morning already? I search around in the covers for my phone. My finger brushes over something sleek and a light shines in my eyes. 9:15pm. A 5 hour nap! Geez, I really was exhausted.

I get up and turn on all the lights in the room. My bathroom door is where I left it, mostly open. The arched door leading down to the basement and my Dad's old office laboratory is shut. My bedroom door is cracked and light is streaming in from the main room. I don't think I turned the lights off. All good so far. I quickly shut my door and lock it. My heart is beating out of my chest from fear but I have no idea why. I'm psyching myself out. With the funeral and all of these life changes, my mind is playing tricks on me. Then I remember Mom's comment last night about a security detail. Was that Tom? Was he my security guy? Why didn't I think to ask him? Maybe he's hanging around outside? Maybe that's who I heard? I calm myself down enough to think somewhat clearly. I need a shower and food.

Twenty minutes later, I literally have to pry myself from that shower. Life changing experience. Who knew water pressure could feel so good. I Door Dash a grain bowl and decide to keep it casual, pajama tank and shorts. I'm not going anywhere. Hopefully I don't offend Tom, assuming he's even around. Then again, maybe I should unpack my robe so I don't scare the delivery person. Mind over matter Catherine, you've got this. I crack open the door to my room and search the hall before I peak around the corner to the main room. The lights are on. I manage to make it to the main room without passing out from fear. My confidence is back. See, nothing. I tune into my surroundings and begin to hear rain lightly tapping against the wall of windows behind me in the main room. Then the doorbell rings. That was fast.

Opening the door, I catch the sight of rain falling at a steady pace around the front porch lights. The rest of the driveway is pitch black at first until my eyes adjust. A car takes off around the circular drive. The delivery driver is taking off already. No town car in the driveway. Hmm, I guess Tom's off the clock. I look down and notice my food package on the stone porch in front of me, rain drops pelting on the brown paper bag. I bend down to rescue my food from the rain and an orange tabby cat comes out of nowhere beside me, rubbing against my leg. "Hey, little one." The cat traces a circular pattern around me as I pet it, her, maybe. The top coat of her fur is wet but she's not drenched. She hasn't been out here long. "Where did you come from, little one? What's your name?" I notice her collar and look at the metal tag.

Ginger

Hmm, creative much? I flip the tag over and it reads:

If found, call Aria (571) 662-9010

Oh, this is Aria's cat! Aria is Charlie's cousin, his Aunt Adeline's only daughter. Aria is beltway royalty. A trust-fund baby and only child of Charlie's Uncle Robert and Aunt Adeline. Uncle Robert, Charlie's Mom's brother, founded Hearst Communications in the late 80's which was bought by Lockheed or Boeing (can't remember which one) for hundreds of millions in 2000 to overhaul their air fleet communication systems. His Uncle Robert died within months of the acquisition and Aria's birth. When Charlie came to live with his Aunt Adeline after his Mom died, Aria was about to enter kindergarten. I used to babysit Aria. She was so adorable, a sweet little girl, and she adored her older cousin like her own brother. But by the time she entered our private school, the lower school, she was welcomed into the popular crowd and her personality changed. Those were social circles Charlie and I weren't welcome around, but then again, we never cared to join them, really. Aria was always a sweet girl growing up, but she had her moments. Uncle Robert's death took its toll on Aunt Adeline and she was a shell of a woman, a shell of a mother, really. It's a miracle Aria turned out as well as she did, honestly. Charlie had quite a bit to do with it, I'm sure. He was always so protective of her. I think he felt a responsibility for her and Aunt A. like he was trying to save them to make up for the loss of his mother.

I enter Aria's number in my phone, snap a quick photo of the cat that is now purring like a revving engine on my lap, and shoot her a quick text.

> Hey, Aria, it's Cat! Is this cute thing yours? Found her on my porch just now. You home? Want to come get her?

I get an immediate reply from Aria.

OMG, Cat, is that really you??!! Miss you so much, girl! We SO need to catch up! That is SO my lil' Ging!! Charlie "Charles" and his entourage are supposed to be watching her. GRRRR!!! Can you bring her back to Charles, please? He's on my shit list! I'm in Paris until next Friday but can't wait to catch up! Love you ▢ p.s. sorry about your Dad ▢

I reply back.

Miss you too girl! Can't wait to catch up! Does Charlie live at your Mom's house? Is that where I should take Ginger? P.S. thank you

She replies immediately.

OMG, you don't know? Charles inherited the house last year. It's his compound now. So weird, I know. Take Ging back to the house. And, please don't judge me when you see it, Cat. I had NOTHING to do with the décor. Gotta go. Thank you!

I reply back.

LOL! No worries at all! Bringing Ging back to Charlie now. Safe travels!

She replies back with a blurry photo of her at an outdoor café, a glass of wine in her hand and a very handsome dude with a beautiful smile by her side. How the hell is she in France in the middle of a pandemic? Isn't travel to Europe completely locked down? And then I remember the time difference – 5 or 6 hours maybe – it's 3am in Paris! What is she doing out at this hour?! Only Aria!

This exchange with Aria has me curious. Charlie *now Charles* inherited his Aunt's house? When did this happen? I check his Instagram page. No posts since his epic experience traveling the globe. I search for his accounts on Twitter and Facebook. Nothing. What did she mean by "his entourage"? Just then it hits me. Maybe he's going by Charles now? I start to try combinations of Hearst and Charles and his middle name. I think it started with the letter D. Yes, his middle initial was D for Draper, I remember because that show *Mad Men* was popular when he first moved here. Again, nothing. The cat starts to stir in my lap and tries to jump away from me. I look down at my takeout package. This is pathetic. I need to get this cat back to Charlie and eat. I lift the cat into my arms and set out for Aunt Adeline's, now Charlie's, "compound".

* * *

PART II

"I sometimes have a queer feeling with regard to you—especially when you are near me, as now: it is as if I had a string somewhere under my left ribs, tightly and inextricably knotted to a similar string situated in the corresponding quarter of your little frame. And if that boisterous Channel, and two hundred miles or so of land come broad between us, I am afraid that cord of communion will be snapt; and then I've a nervous notion I should take to bleeding inwardly." –Mr. Rochester

7. CHARLES

Life can be so fucking ironic. I'm hammering out one
last mile on the treadmill replaying conversations from
today's meetings with FDA, CDC and White House leaders –
the biggest single day in Mayvin's 27 year history – and it happens
to be the same fucking day Dr. Mayvin, who unknowingly invented the miracle vaccine 15 years ago in his basement laboratory, is being buried six feet under. I know about life's little iron-
ies, believe me. I'm living proof the universe has a sick sense of
humor when she wants to. Catch her on an off moment and she'll
flip you the finger in the worst of ways. Well, at least he didn't die
of the virus. That would be ironic. Man Dies in Pandemic, Never
to Discover He Invented The Cure to The Virus that Killed Him

I just wish he were here to witness all this. To be the object of
everyone's praise and gratitude, to have all the glory. I'm an im-
poster and a thief, only succeeding in packaging up his brilliance
and making it all usable to someone. This one just happened to
be useful to the entire human race. I always believed in his genius. If there was one person in the world who I knew, deep down,
was truly brilliant, it was Mayvin. Brilliant but completely misunderstood and undervalued. When I came back from my global
trek after discovering and honing my meditative super powers, I
had devised a plan to pay retribution for my sick fuck up that day
in Nepal.

Before I left, Mayvin had been working on a technology that
could see into the earth, but further than any other existing tech-

nology. Like ground penetrating radar, only much better. Despite his deteriorating mind, his science was sound, his math seemed accurate, but the application wasn't right. We couldn't actually *see* anything. I knew the technology would be invaluable if perfected. I was in the middle of one of my trips to the deep when the solution came to me. I knew in an instant exactly what we needed to make the technology work. I came back to work for Mayvin as soon as I returned from Nepal. I remember searching through published engineering papers and checking Google the entire trip back to be sure no one had cracked the code. I was so nervous someone would beat us to it.

When I shared my discovery with Mayvin, I caught him in a lucid moment and he knew I had solved his hardest puzzle. I swear he could have kissed me. He was elated. We made a good team. But when I went to Mayvin's legal team to file the patent, they shared with me the company was in dire financial straits due to some lost contracts and mismanagement since Mayvin's mental decline.

So, I leveraged everything I owned, namely my recently inherited 20 acres of prime real estate from my Mom's brother's estate, and bought a minority share of Mayvin Enterprises. I would never take control. The company would stay in Catherine's family, I owed that to her. With my capital, we were able to keep the company out of trouble until we could patent the technology and design the military prototypes. In the span of five months, the company landed contracts valuing more than it had made in its entire history. This was December of last year. That's when Mayvin appointed me the next CEO.

By January he had stopped talking and the light was gone from his eyes. I knew it was only a matter of time. I promised him I would take care of the company and provide for Catherine and her Mom, that they would want for nothing. By that time, news of Catherine's divorce was common knowledge and my plan to keep my feelings for her eternally buried was becoming more difficult.

Not that I was doing anything about it, Catherine had enough on her hands with the miscarriage, law school and that fucker getting his ass lost in Syria.

I would visit Mayvin almost every night. I'd leave the office late, head to the house, workout and meditate and then walk over to the Mayvin's. Catherine's Mom always had a dinner plate ready to heat up for me. I'd eat while I shared the day's company news with him never knowing if he actually comprehended a word I was saying. One day it just burst out of me. I confided in him that I was in love with his daughter, that I loved her more than it was possible for any human being to love another. It felt good, freeing, to finally say the words out loud. But I'm a coward, waiting until the man was practically a vegetable to share with him the depth of my feelings for his daughter.

* * *

The treadmill begins to slow down and I can hear my phone buzzing on the dock. It's Syd, my head of security who's currently living in my annex with all of this Syria shit going down and the press following me. He's an Aussie. I met him in Sydney, where he grew up, about half way through my epic journey to "find myself" and we hit it off. His name's actually Rorey, but I call him Syd for obvious reasons. "Syd, what's up?" "Hey Chuck, sorry to bug you on your run, but I thought you should know. She's left her house on foot and headed in this direction. In the rain." "Fuck, seriously?" I'm not ready for this.

"The cameras don't lie, dude." "I'm not ready for this yet, Syd. I thought I had another 24 hours to get my head straight before she sees me and figures everything out." "I don't know what to tell you man, grow a pair though. And you better hurry, 'cause she's almost at the front door. Then again, I'd be perfectly happy to answer it for you, man. She's smokin'." "No!" I bark, a little too quickly. "No, I've got it, Syd. Talk about her like that again and

I'll cut your balls off, asshole." He laughs into the phone. "Chuck, man. Reelaaax dude. I was just teasing you. Oh, and by the way, make sure she knows there's some scary evil military sect in Syria trying to use her to blackmail us for technology that sees through the earth, okay? Maybe she'll avoid traipsing around in the dark in skimpy booty shorts and no bra for a while until we've got this one figured out." And at that comment, I let out a frustrated growl, my temper raging, grab a towel and run up the back stairs.

A million thoughts are flying through my head. She knows. That's why she's here. She knows I bought her Dad's company and she's pissed at me for not telling her. Fuck! This is not how I planned it to go down. I can't have her angry with me yet. Maybe she doesn't know. I've deliberately tried to stay out of the press. How would she know I've changed my name? We haven't talked in months. Keep it together, Draper. I leap up the top three stairs and can just make out her frame coming up the driveway. Fuck! What is she wearing? Next to fucking nothing. Is she serious? Celia promised me she was going to share with her there were complications right now and she needed to be careful. To stay safe. Strutting around in next-to-nothing in the middle of the night is *not safe*, Catherine. I'm at the front door in less than two strides. I throw the towel over my bare shoulder and throw open the front door with the force of my anger over her carelessness just as she approaches the other side of it, finger on the door bell. I don't even think, just instinctively grab her by the wrist and pull her inside, inches from me as I slam the door behind her. She lets out a squeal as I pull her wrist towards me and something jumps from her arms into the house. She was carrying something. A cat? Oh, that damn orange cat. How'd she get Aria's cat? I'm panting all of a sudden, why am I panting? *This is not staying cool, Draper. You're being a control freak.*

I look down at her, still gripping her wrist. She's staring at my chest. Shit, in my haste I forgot to put my shirt on. I take a deep breath and begin to register that she's in front of me, in the flesh.

I take her in. Every inch of her. She's wet from the rain. Her straw-berry blond hair is unruly *like it always is* and cascading down her shoulders, a few strands dripping raindrops down her arm. Her pink lips are slightly parted and perfect. Her neck is bare, soft and porcelain. God, I remember her beautiful neckline. I used to fantasize about kissing up and down her throat. I would lick and suck her there until she started to come undone and then I would move my attentions lower and lower. *Only in your fucking dreams, you pervert.* I start to loosen my grip on her wrist and softly move my fingers up her arm while I continue my scan of her gor-geous body. She's wearing a robe, very short, it's come undone at the waist and is falling away from her shoulders. Her camisole is barely covering the tops of her breasts and I can see her nipples hardening through the thin cotton as my eyes linger a few seconds longer. Her sculpted thighs curve out from her tiny cotton shorts and my free hand flexes compulsively with a desire to touch her there. She never stopped running. My visual seduction is inter-rupted by the sound of her voice.

"Charlie?" she questions, scanning her eyes up my body and stop-ping at my eyes. I meet her gaze. Well, she called me Charlie, and she doesn't sound upset. Hopefully, I'm in the clear one more night. But I'm still angry with her. Walking all this way in the rain. It's practically a mile between our houses and up my drive-way. Syd would have to open the gate, too. Bastard. He didn't mention that. "Charlie?" she questions again. I stare into her eyes again and blink. This woman is a goddess. I want to lean in and kiss her perfect lips. I blink again and my brain finally starts to register she's asked me a question. "Yes." I manage to blurt out ra-ther pathetically before I manage to grab a hold of my senses and act like a human being. "Yes, Catherine, it's me." I start again with a slight edge this time. And suddenly my anger at her disregard for her own safety and the fact that she just flashed every perfect inch of her bare flesh to my entire security team and whomever else managed to be driving down our street takes hold of me, fueling my angry tone. "What are you doing here, Catherine? It's pouring down rain, it's late and you're very underdressed. This is not safe, Catherine, hasn't your mother shared with you what's going on? This is not being, careful!" I bite out through my teeth, practically growling at her. Her eyes get wide and a flash of anger registers in her cheeks. Shit, I wish I had a do over.

"Well, hello to you too. It's nice to be greeted with such warmth by my old friend after, what? Seven years of not seeing him?" I blink at her and frown. Fuck. Way to make a first impression, Draper.

"In fact, I'm not sure it *is* you, Charlie. You've changed. You're different. Physically ... different. And rude, too. My old friend was not rude and he didn't look like-" I grab her wrist again and stop her. I don't want to hear – I can't bear to hear what she might say.

"Didn't look like what, Catherine? What *did* your dear friend, Charlie, look like? Small? Thin? Weak?" I wait for her to respond. I'm on a roll now. Angry at what happened. What I wasn't able to be for her from the beginning. She replies shyly, responding instinctively to my scolding tone and removing her wrist from my grasp at the same time.

"No. That's not what he was like. He was sweet and charming and I liked the way he looked."

Oh, sure she did. That's why her response is utterly lacking in the description department. We stare at each other in silence. I don't know where I want to go next with her. Devour her mouth or chide at her some more. She decides for me.

"Aria's cat came to my door." She says seemingly out of the blue. I turn my head to question her. "That's why I'm here. To return Aria's cat."

"Oh." I manage to reply in a softer tone this time. "Thank you. She must have escaped again when the housekeeper left." She looks up at me like I'm an alien. Somehow my inner-Charlie finds his way to the surface. My fingers clench and then find their way to the back of my neck. My old nervous tick.

"Listen, Catherine, I'm sorry. I'm being rude, you're right. It was a long day with the feds on the vaccine breakthrough and I'm just worried about your safety. Forgive me? Please?" I plead with her. My sorry Charlie eyes in full effect.

"Of course, I understand. It's been a long day for me too-" I cut her off again, now feeling like a complete asshole. The fucking funeral. How could I forget?!

"Oh my god, Catherine. I'm so sorry. The funeral. Are you okay? It went well?" She's staring at my chest again, looking at me like I'm an alien. Yep, I've changed. You got me on that one. These abs were definitely not there in high school. I'll give you that. And I'm suddenly worried she may not like what she sees. This is maddening. Everything is so clear when I'm meditating. In person, in the flesh, it's blurry.

"Oh no, no worries!" she replies prying her eyes from my body and looking up at me finally. "The funeral went really well. It's just … tough. You know how it is. I don't need to tell you. *She's referring to the fact that I had lost both of my parents by my 12th birthday.* But it was good, really good. And my Mom was brilliant. As always."

"Of course she was and I'm sure you were too, Catherine. I'm sure you held the day together. I know you. I'm so sorry again that I couldn't be there. Tomorrow, though. Tomorrow, I promise we'll celebrate him together." I'm staring at her. Trying to get her to look at me, really look at me. She's shy. Her eyes are looking down at the floor. Why, I wonder?

"Listen, I better go." She says softly staring down into her clasped hands, wringing finger against finger.

"Oh no you don't." I hold out my hand to her as if to stop her from leaving. "I'll drive you back home. Just wait here while I grab my shirt." I don't give her a chance to protest and run down the stairs to grab my shirt. I'm back before either of us can blink and she's still in her same spot staring at the floor, hands wringing. This time she's biting her lip and I can't resist the urge to touch her. I reach out and softly lift her chin with my thumb and index finger. She looks up at me, defiant but sweet. My Catherine. "Hi." I say to her. As if it's my truce for us to start over. "Hi." She says back and I imagine it's her accepting my truce. I wink at her and she smiles. Do over it is then!

"Come, the garage is down the hall. Let's get you home."

8. CATHERINE

Holy. Fucking. Shit. Where is my friend, Charlie, and what have you done with him? Seriously? Who is this man I'm following to his garage? This cannot be the same Charlie. I'm so embarrassed. I've been ogling him since the second I walked through the door. Why did no one prepare me for this? I blame my Mom. She could have at least alluded to the fact that he'd changed. Good lord, he's hot! I hate to even use that word. It's so cliché. I've never been the type of girl who could be attracted to a guy for looks alone. But, I mean, sometimes you have to call it like you see it. I think back to our track meets and Charlie in his running shorts, shirt off. It's like his cuteness factor just grew and grew and now the needle is pointing firmly on Hot! He's in running shorts and now a grey dry-fit tee, hugging all that muscular glory, and some kind of space-age running shoes. All of this physical awareness has me checking my own attire. I sheepishly grab the sides of my robe and tie it firmly together. I'm soaked from the rain. My stomach growls and I remember I have take-out back on the porch. The porch. Shit, I think I left the door open. Mr. Grumpy-pants leading the way to his garage won't like that much, will he? Maybe he won't notice. This entire encounter has been weird since the second he literally pulled me through the front door. He had me in some kind of trance with his stare. My body was like a puppet on a string, responding to the intensity of his eyes. My arm still feels branded from the heat of his palm. I look down and rub my other hand along my forearm surprised there's not a big red C charred on my wrist.

"Here we are!" He prompts as the passenger door to a - Tesla, maybe? – opens toward me without warning. How'd he do that? He holds the door for me, as if he had been the one to open it, while I scoot myself into the dreamy white leather interior seat. I glance over at the T symbol on the steering wheel. Oh, this is a Tesla. I was right. I've always wanted to drive one of these! I look all around and into the back seat. It looks like a sports car. Gorgeous. Good for Elon Musk. This shit is the bomb. The driver's side door opens and the car sounds like a spaceship about to take off. I peer over and suddenly Charlie, I mean Charles, is staring at me. "Hi." He says so sweetly, I could melt. "Hi." I squeak back at him. "Like what you see?" Suddenly I'm panicked. He's noticed me staring at him for the last ten minutes. This is so embarrassing. What do I say? Wait, does he mean the car? "Elon Musk's a genius. Am I right?" "Oh, the car." I reply, relieved. "Completely. It's gorgeous. Really. How does it drive?" He turns to me and gives me the most beautiful, shit-eating grin. "Like a dream." He replies staring straight into my eyes. Fuck. A wave washes over me and I'm suddenly flushed. Fuck, this is intense. I haven't seen this guy in seven years and I feel like I might combust from pure lust with one look.

He snaps his head away to start driving and his right hand flexes mid-air before it settles on his thigh with a death grip. What is up with that hand? It's like it might reach out and grab me if I'm not careful. Suddenly the garage door whips open and the spaceship sound starts again. We're moving slowly at first and then that hand moves from his thigh to cover my waist like a seatbelt and then he floors it down the driveway in reverse. It's exhilarating but I can see how I would be carsick by now if he wasn't holding me in place. At the end of his driveway, he quickly swings the car into position and switches into drive. I look down at his arm still holding my chest before the car begins to move forward and his head swings in my direction as if to check my reaction. Our eyes meet again for the hundredth time tonight and my entire body turns flush. I notice movement from his seat and look down to see him adjusting his position, his right hand now shielding my view. He begins asking me a question, distracting me.

"So, are you glad to be home, Catherine?" Oh. Why do I register that as such a loaded question? I look down at my lap, suddenly embarrassed that he knows everything I've been through this year. The miscarriage, the wedding, the divorce, Curt leaving for Syria – my life's a fucking disaster and he appears to have his life together here looking like a god among men. How to reply? "Umm, yeah, I think I am. Ready to start fresh. A new chapter." I look up to see his reply as he places the car into park but can see he's staring at my front door which is hanging wide open. Shit. He's gonna freak, isn't he? He hangs his head in front of the steering wheel. "Catherine … " He begins in his now familiar cold, sharp tone. "… you left the door hanging wide open." "I did?" I lie. Oh shit, he's pissed. His eyes are closed and his right hand is in a fist now, knuckles white. Without warning he jumps out of the car and races over to my side, door open, and grabs my hand to lead me to the front door.

He pulls me into the foyer, grabbing my takeout bag on his way in, sets it on the counter and turns to face me. He moves to grab ahold of my shoulders and at first I'm frozen in shock at how comfortable he is with me after all this time that he can reach out and touch me. "I'm going to search the house, top to bottom, okay? It will take me a while. Don't move. Stay right here. For your safety, okay?" He orders me. Initial shock over, I instinctively shrug away from his grasp, not liking being treated like a child. He understands, I can tell. "Cat, it's for your safety. Answer me. You'll stay here, won't move?" I look up at him in defiance, angry that I'm being handled, coddled. I shake my head yes, nevertheless. "Good girl." He says as he grabs my hand and squeezes it to reassure me. "I'll try to be quick."

Good girl? Who does he think he is, anyway? I'm not a child. I'm a grown woman and he's not my keeper. I don't even know him anymore. With every passing minute I get more and more agitated. This is ridiculous. I'm soaked in these clothes. Standing here waiting for him to search my house. It's not that big. Not like that monstrosity he's living in. What's taking him so long? I can't take it anymore. I'm cold and starting to shiver from my wet clothes and I have to pee. I peak around for signs of him but nothing. So, I make a run for my bedroom. He's not there either. I shut my bedroom door and pick out a dry top and shorts and lay them on the bed before I head to the bathroom to pee and dry off. I grab a towel from the rack, slip off my tank top and begin to dry my chest. My thoughts turn to earlier, standing in Charlie's foyer. The way he was staring at me, his eyes piercing through me and the way my body reacted. Such intensity and after we've spent so many years apart. It's unnerving how he is so different but his presence feels so familiar at the same time. I catch sight of something move through the reflection in the mirror and my eyes are pinned in place, my body frozen in fear once again tonight.

A figure begins to appear and familiar rich, velvety brown eyes are staring back at me, at my reflection. I suddenly become aware that my shirt is off, the towel draping from my arm and my cheeks instantly heat and blush. I quickly cover myself up turning in his direction to face him when I should be running into the shower to hide. Our eyes catch again, now face to face from across the room. He's staring at me as he approaches the middle of my bedroom and he's speaking but not to me, someone's talking to him through an earpiece I think. "So, all good on your end? Footage all clear?" He pauses, eyes still glued on my reflection. "Okay, good. All set here too. What's that?" He laughs. "Umm, yeah. It's all good. No. Not yet, at least."

I notice the basement door is ajar and it registers he must have been searching Dad's old laboratory for the would-be intruder he's so concerned about. He begins to speak again, this time to me, as he makes his way toward my bed. I'm still in shock, not able to move for some strange reason and surprised he's not heading toward the door to leave. Then I notice he's heading toward me, my clean shirt in hand, and begin to register what he's saying. "... the coast is clear, so to speak. You should be good, nothing to worry about tonight. But, please keep the doors locked and no more nightly strolls until we have this issue sorted out." Our eyes are locked on each other again. I'm in a trance, feet glued to the floor. The intensity is too much. I'm so drawn to his presence. As he approaches, I hug the towel closer to my body. He acknowledges my shyness and drapes the clean shirt across my shoulders to cover me further, his eyes still commanding mine. His fingertips blanch my left shoulder and I shudder with goosebumps. Then, he breaks eye contact leaning into my ear. "You take my breath away." He whispers.

At his words, goosebumps spread further down my body and my knees forget to stay straight. I falter, trying to catch myself against the bathroom vanity but his reflexes are quicker than mine, his hand catches around my arm to stabilize me. He flashes me that megawatt smile and in the next moment he's heading toward my bedroom door to leave.

On the way out the door, he turns and says casually "Looking forward to tomorrow. Hopefully both of us can manage to keep our shirts on." He winks at me and then he's gone.

9. CATHERINE

I make it to bed a little after 11pm and I still haven't recovered from the awkward encounter with Charlie. I'm tossing and turning, plagued by emotions. I'm embarrassed by my body's reaction to him and my ineptness and inability to form two coherent words in his presence. I'm completely puzzled by the change in his physical appearance. How is that even possible? I'm still trying to figure out what Aria meant by his entourage. Did she mean the housekeeper he alerted to and the security guy he was talking to on the phone, or something more? I'm so curious about how and when he inherited that house and what's the story behind the renovation. It looks like Tony Stark's compound. But most of all, I'm pissed beyond reason and completely freaked out at this whole security concern. And I'm more angry at myself for not being able to think on my feet in Charlie's presence and demand a more detailed explanation, or shut the damn door instead of standing there like a complete idiot with my shirt off.

I guess he goes by Charles now, according to Aria. I wonder how much he interacts with the CEO, the other Charles. He seemed to know more than I would have guessed and what does he do at Mayvin that he's talking to the security guy after hours? About me?! Sleep is impossible. I squeeze my eyes shut, punch the pillow and try to divert my attention from the two Charles's who have suddenly taken over my life and have me completely on edge.

10. CHARLES

I barely make it back into the garage and I'm fuming, I'm so pissed with myself at how I handled this first encounter with Catherine. I completely gave away my physical attraction to her. I practically jumped on her on three separate occasions in a 15-minute span of time tonight. And the bathroom encounter. Fuck! I hope she doesn't have any idea how close I came to scooping her up, throwing her on the bed and having my way with her. God Charles, you sound like a fucking depraved brute. Who thinks like that other than some kind of obsessed loser? And what kind of cheesy inappropriate comment was that at the end. Could I have made that more awkward for her? Something about seeing her, my body just took over and the sane part of my brain didn't stand a fucking chance. Tomorrow's going to be a nightmare if I can't control my urge to touch her, to kiss her, to just be next to her every fucking second. I can't think like this or act like this. She doesn't feel the way I do, yet. She probably never will. And the security shit. She's completely confused. I didn't stop to explain anything to her. I was overcome by anger at her lack of attention to her own safety – mad terrorist extortionist threat aside – and couldn't calm down for a second to explain anything to her. Would have been a good time to do that after I searched the house but then she was standing there with her breasts on full display and my fucking libido took over again.

I try to set my thoughts aside for a second, running through my mental list of things I was supposed to do tonight before her unexpected visit. Review the final edits to tomorrow night's tribute video, prep for the follow up calls with the two remaining pharmaceutical manufacturers, eat dinner, feed Aria's cat. I storm in from the garage door and decide to take these in reverse order. I fill the food bowl by the fridge and an orange ball of fur begins to saunter in my direction. I give her a swift pet and open the fridge to find my meal ready to heat and then head upstairs to prep for tomorrow's meetings while I eat. The video can wait for the morning. I don't need any more reminders of Catherine to distract my thoughts tonight.

An hour's gone by and I'm spinning my wheels. I can manage to concentrate in 30 second increments before every beautiful inch and curve of her body, head to toe, seeps into my thoughts. This is madness. The literal definition of insanity. I should run over there now and just get it over with. Tell her everything. That I'm an enlightened savant. That I've missed her. That I left to travel the world so I could find myself and be something better for her one day. That I've been obsessed with her, in love with her, since I was 11 years old. That my abilities got her pregnant, that it was me and not Curt. That I saved her Dad's company from ruin to make amends for what I did to her. That the only thing I wish for in life is for her to one day love me back with just an ounce of the love I feel for her. You know, it's so ironic. Only me, Charles Hearst Draper, would develop and hone this singular impressive mental and spiritual subconscious skill and continue to be a fucking emotional, obsessive, controlling basket-case in my conscious life. I shut my laptop and head down to the meditation chamber, determined to regain some equilibrium before tomorrow.

11. CHARLES

It doesn't take me long. Within minutes I find weightlessness, the feeling of oneness with my surroundings I now find so familiar. Instantly my mind finds her and goes to her like all the times before, but this time the pull is much stronger. Like the first time, the pull is almost impossible to resist. I'm beside her bed and she's sleeping, barely. She's restless. Tossing and turning. Before I can register my movement, I'm lying beside her stroking her hair. It's like all those years ago. The last time - the only time - we touched. I am the earth beneath me, the sky above me and all the elements in the house are moving along with me. Every stroke of her hair is like ecstasy. I feel pure unadulterated love. Her physical closeness to me in the conscious world is making it hard for me to resist the urge to be one with her, but I maintain the mental control and overcome it, just barely. The consequences are too great. She's calm now, her body still and content. Her breathing is even. She sighs, a long beautiful, peaceful mew. But then she begins to call my name like a whispering question on her tongue. Her lips are parted and my name seeps through ever so softly. "Charlie?" she whispers over and over. Then her body begins to move rhythmically under the covers as she beckons for me with her mouth and I'm lost. All control out the fucking window. Yani didn't prepare me for this.

She calls for me again and I move closer to her, holding her now. "I'm here Catherine. It's me". She moves from between us and cuddles into me. "Touch me, Charlie." I move to stroke her face this time. Gently, again and again, with the back of my hand. She can feel the state I'm in. I know this at least, from Yani. My enlightened mental state is heightening her experience as well. She is with me on my trip. Her dream-state movements are erotic and beautiful. It's taking all the control I have not to act on my physical urges. The desire to be inside her is like no other. She begins to touch me. My hair. My face. My arms. I'm about to explode from pleasure. "You've changed ..." She whispers. "... but you're still the same. So familiar. Like home." I continue to caress her face and she slides my hand down further to her chest. "Touch me like before ... before I left." I pause and wait before I act, seizing some control, the elements breathing in and out with me.

The earth, the sky, the fresh water lakes and the ocean miles away all swaying and breathing with me. Everything feels right, less troubled. She's so right, it's like home. She's like home and she's with me and we're breathing in unison together, her in her dream-like state and me in my enlightened state. It feels right. And then before I can begin, her hand is moving mine along her body. I take control and move over her caressing the curve of her breasts one at a time and then in unison. She reaches up as if to kiss me and I meet her half-way. It's like a spark ignites in the air around us. My control continues to fade and my mouth finds her neck, licking and sucking. I move slowly down her neck and chest until I again find the swells of her breasts and the peaks of her nipples, hard and swollen, waiting for my touch. She's writhing beneath me to the rhythm of our breathing and I place my hand on her hip, stroking her and holding her to tame her movements, lest we end this game right now with another fateful mistake. She arches up and I take the hint, enveloping one of her breasts with my mouth, sucking, lapping, nipping, tugging to the sound of her erotic mews. I move from one breast to the next alternating between my mouth and my hands, not able to resist her beauty and the effect my attentions have on her. My control is continuing to fade, her presence and closeness nearly impossible to keep from drawing her in and becoming one with me and my universe. My mouth moves along the beautiful porcelain skin of her belly, continuing to lick and suck as I begin to lift away from her. She senses my movement and grabs ahold of my back to draw me closer. "Please, Charlie." She pleads. "You feel so good, I need you. Please" she continues. Oh, dear God. I need to leave her presence but we continue our syncopated breathing rhythm and removing my subconscious from this experience becomes impossible.

She's in a full out dream sequence and I'm in a leading role. She continues pleading and lifts up to remove her panties, the words please and Charlie kissing her lips. Every urge, desire, dream and fantasy since I hit puberty has been some erotic combination of the scene before me and I'm struggling for control. She's dreaming. She wants pleasure. From me, no less. How can I deny her? My subconscious urge wins over and my face dives between her legs, parting them slowly, my mouth kissing up her inner thighs, alternating left to right and back again until I reach her beautiful glistening flower, wet, dripping for my attention. I gently kiss the top of her mound and she begins stroking my hair, fingers entangling, pulling and stroking with the intensity of her need. My hands lift her behind and with one long stroke of my tongue she comes undone, lost in her pleasure, my name like a prayer on her lips. I am lost too, in the beauty of her undoing, continuing to lap and lick and suck at her as she pulsates on my tongue, reveling in my place as the object of her desire, in her dream, at least. I force myself to end the experience with a pang of loss, pulling her panties and covers back in place. I chastely kiss her forehead, whispering "sweet dreams" before I will my subconscious to leave her presence, once again, praying for the day when I can stay, forever.

12. CATHERINE

I wake slowly to the sound of birds singing melodically outside my window, light streaming through the slats of my blinds. I feel rested. Really rested. Comfortable and dreamy but with a bolt of energy like I could take on the world. I stretch and begin to rise stopping to prop myself up on my elbows for a second and think. I had a dream last night. A really good dream. About Charlie! Oh. My. God. The entire dream sequence begins to piece together in my mind. I had a wet dream about Charlie. This is not good. What is happening to me? The stress of this year and the shock of coming back to find my high school best friend is now god's gift to women has my subconscious doing wacky things. Well, this is embarrassing! Put this out of your mind, Catherine. Hopefully I can manage to keep it out of my mind the next time I see him too. Tonight! Oh God, I have to see him tonight. This is awkward. Maybe if I fill my day with very serious, adult-like things I can manage to get through tonight without an impure thought.

I head into the main room and flip on the TV as I make my way to the kitchen to find some coffee, pleased when I see a Keurig machine and a tray of pods next to it. I'm still in my peaceful, I-had-an-orgasm-in-my-sleep-last-night state when the voice on the news channel begins to register in my consciousness

" ... EO of Mayvin Enterprises, Charles Draper, met with US HHS officials at the White House yesterday to discuss plans for mass production and widespread distribution of the cure-all vaccine developed by Mayvin's subsidiary, B.H. Mayvin Laboratories, earl-

ier this month. The CEO confirmed that the company consulted with the White House prior to down-selecting two large US-based pharmaceutical manufacturers to handle this critical production effort with the plan for all Americans to have access to the vaccine by Christmas. Mayvin Laboratories is currently producing enough vaccines to handle life-threatening cases in ICUs across the country. Draper is slated to meet with health officials in the UK, the EU and China next week to chart a path forward for global distribution."

My jaw drops and I'm staring at the screen hoping to see an image of Mayvin or the CEO or my Dad, maybe, but it's just a graphic of the virus under a microscope and the news anchor. The news cuts to commercial with weather up next. For some reason the gravity of what has just occurred, at what Mayvin has accomplished hasn't yet sunk in until this moment. This is huge. HUGE. And I own this company, or will, at least. What do I know about running a business, period, let alone a defense business, let alone a biomedical laboratory that just hit the big time. Well, okay, I'm just the shareholder. I just need to make sure the right people are in place to run it, right? This is overwhelming. Suddenly I'm extremely nervous to meet Charles. He's really made quite a mark on the company in a few short months as CEO. My Dad chose well, really well. He must be brilliant. I hope he doesn't see me as the privileged trust-fund baby he's now got to deal with as his new boss, because that is not what this is. I pick up my phone to scroll through the news app. I need to find out more about Mayvin, the vaccine and Charles Draper. Dead center on my screen is a notification of an email from Charles H. Draper with the subject: Memorial Gala in Honor of Dr. Blanton H. Mayvin, Jr. Spooky. It's like he knew I was about to stalk him on Google. I open the message and it's a beautiful digital invitation to tonight's memorial dinner with fine scroll-like print and the perfect black and white image of my Dad seated in his laboratory, looking very debonair and deep in thought. I wish I could reach through the screen and hug him. If he only knew what he had helped create. Oh Daddy, I miss you.

I save the invitation to my screen and continue my mission to do a little research. There is quite a bit about the vaccine and Mayvin. Apparently, we launched a technology that can see through the earth in December and won a ton of military contracts. Now that's Tony Stark shit! I couldn't find much of anything on the CEO though. I guess it's because Mayvin's not public? I sigh. Tonight will be here soon enough and I can finally meet this mystery man. It's time for a run! I haven't been able to run the rail trail behind my house in over a year. Every time I came home before it was all about seeing Dad or, most recently, dealing with the pregnancy. I pause and my thoughts settle on how different things would be right now if I hadn't miscarried. Would we have stayed married? Would I be here now, visiting, with a newborn? So strange the sharp turns our lives take.

The rail trail run didn't disappoint. It never does. I can now see my life coming into view, my future still uncertain and unknown but, at least now, after 6 miles of running meditation, the unknown doesn't seem so scary or intimidating. I'm a Mayvin. I got this! I shower and head to the grocery store to pick up some staples for lunch and it's only when I walk back through the door with arms full of groceries that I realize I've got nothing to wear tonight. I check the time, it's 3pm. Shit, how could I overlook such a *minor* detail. And then I think back to Charlie's comment about keeping our shirts on and I blush. No need to go there again, Catherine. I vaguely remember my Mom saying something about a personal shopper. So over the top, but boy do I hope that is actually the case right about now. She answers on a half ring like she knew I was about to call. "Hi honey! All ready for tonight? Did you get the invitation? I made Charles send one to you so you could see how beautiful it was. "

"I did, Mom, it's really lovely. Charles or whomever prepared it did a really nice job."

"That picture of your Dad. Charles pulled it from an old archive at the office from the early days. I had completely forgotten we'd taken those. But anyway, I'm sure that's not why you're calling."

"Well, actually Mom, I totally forgot to get something to wear tonight and I see it's a black tie thing and ..."

"Oh, honey, don't go any further. I completely forgot to tell you, the dresses from the personal shopper are hanging in the hall closet. In my haste to get the house cleared and ready I just ran them into the front hall. There should be a bag of shoes too. I don't think I told them your shoe size but if they don't fit, maybe you have something in what you packed?"

"I'm sure I'll figure it out Mom, thank you. I'm breathing a sigh of relief that I at least have something to wear."

"Oh, don't thank me. Charles thought of everything. He knew with you heading back from school and the exam and the funeral it would be too difficult to side-track you with these trivial things."

"Well that was very thoughtful of him." I manage in an annoyed, flat tone, all praise for him from earlier completely snuffed out now with this creepy personal gesture. That's it. I don't care what he's done for this company, he just sounds weird and over the top. I don't like him. Sight unseen.

"I've gotta run to the salon for my hair appointment. See you tonight. The car should be coming for you 30 minutes before the cocktail hour. Details should be in Charles's email."

"Okay, Mom. Sounds good. See you tonight." I say robotically, ready to be off the phone so I can stew some more of this personal shopper business and the security mystery. I don't like this guy and I don't trust him.

I put the groceries away, make a turkey wrap with hummus and chips and clean up before I head to the hall and unveil my wardrobe options for the evening. The hanging bag is in the front hall closet exactly where mom said it would be. There's a white folded piece of paper in a plastic sleeve on the front of the bag. I pull the paper out and unfold it. It's an email exchange between the Nordstrom shopper, Danika Price, and Charles Draper. Danika Price. That sounds a bit like a stripper's name, kind of. Maybe he's having a fling with the personal shopper. Maybe that's why he was so hell bent on ordering me dresses for my Dad's memorial, helping his lover out under the guise that it was to relieve my stress. I read the email exchange from start to finish starting with the second page.

From: charles.draper@mayvin.com
To: danika.price@dcpersonalshoppers.com

Subject: Special Request

Hey Price, Got a special request for you. But first, gotta say, spot on with the new running shoes. I just read an article about the carbonplate technology and then a pair shows up in my closet the next day. Amazing. You read my mind.

So, the special request. You know the details on the memorial gala I'm holding in honor of the founder of my company next week? I need an evening gown, shoes, accessories, the whole works for a very special guest of honor.

She's mid-20s, long strawberry-blond hair, fair skinned with a touch of freckles. She loves the classics. Her style is simple and elegant. 5 ft 7. She was a size 4 before college but she's more muscular now, toned, a runner. Use your judgment on size. Might need a few options. Shoe size, 8, but in running shoes. Might not translate to heels.

Let me know if that's enough to get you started. Oh, I need the wardrobe delivered to Celia Mayvin, 610 Elmhurst Drive in McLean.

Charles H. Draper
CEO | Mayvin Enterprises, Inc.

From: danika.price@dcpersonalshoppers.com
To: charles.draper@mayvin.com

RE: Special Request

Charles,

Consider it done. I know just the designer.

Glad you like the shoes!

Danika

Danika Price
Wardrobe Consultant
DC Personal Shoppers
Exclusive shoppers for Nordstrom & Saks 5th Ave Customers

The papers slide from my fingers gliding like feathers to the hard-wood. At first I'm confused, feeling completely violated reading such a personal description of myself. Then it hits me like a ton of bricks. How did I not see this? How did I not put two and two together until now? Charles. Draper. Charlie. I bend down to scoop up the papers again. Staring at the email. Staring at his signature block, his email address. Charles H. Draper, CEO. Charles is Charlie. Charlie is Charles. I think back to every conversation I had with my mother over the last 9 months since Dad got ill. She always referred to him as Charles. *Our* Charles.

"Charles came to visit your Dad again tonight, Catherine. He comes every night. He shares every detail about the day with him, Catherine. He was always so dedicated and loyal. A dear friend to your father, to our family."

Why didn't she tell me? He was *my* best friend. I spent nearly every waking hour with him for six straight years and she can't bring herself to tell me this? She didn't think to explain? Maybe she thought I knew he'd changed his name.

Why did he change his name? That's so weird. Maybe to go with his new body?

Maybe she assumed I've been in touch with him all this time.

Oh god! Last night. Standing in front of the mirror, naked!
His whisper in my ear.
My dream.
How he's changed.
That compound he built.

Why is he running my Dad's company? Wait, Mom indicated something with the trust paperwork about another shareholder. Yes, it was about Charles having to take a small stake in the company due to some kind of financial *wrinkle* she called it.

I read the email through again, hanging on every word. Charlie *is* Charles. Only Charlie would know these details about me. My running shoe size – from high school track. I like the classics – I practically bored him to tears every afternoon with my recitations from 18th century literature.

Why is he doing all of this? Who does he think he is, taking over my life like this? He hasn't even thought to call me once to talk about any of this?! Why the mystery? I think back on the *very few* text exchanges we've had in the last year. My birthday. But that was before he became CEO. *Just to say that to myself is unreal.* Then, nothing. Nothing until the day of the bar exam. *Seriously?* My Dad appointed him. That would have happened, right? Daddy wasn't in his right mind. Would Charlie take advantage of my Dad like that? I mean he's 25, no, maybe 26 now? No one in their right mind names a 26-year-old their new CEO. What is Charlie thinking? I am *so* mad at him! And all that awkwardness yesterday. The flirting. The weird chemistry between us. He couldn't manage to say anything about this to me? The security concern. Mayvin's been tracking the search mission for Curt. Is Charles behind this? Has he been tracking my ex-husband?

He's been playing new member of the Mayvin family for the last year, maybe longer for God's sake! I'm pacing the hallway now. Completely fucking losing my shit over this. I'll call him. Right now. I'll give him a piece of my mind. Keeping all this from me. What the hell? I don't need protected from important details about my life, Charlie, *Charles*, whoever you fucking are!

No, I can't call him right now. I'm too angry. I need to calm down, gather my thoughts. I'll go over there, to his *compound*. Confront him to his face. His compound. Wait. Oh God. What is Mayvin paying him? Is he getting rich off my company and can't even talk to me? This is disgusting. My hands are shaking. I pick up my phone and dial my Mom. It rings over and over before the automated message begins. Figures. I dial again. Five times in a row and she still doesn't pick up. Mom!

What to do? I can't go tonight. No. Way. He's made me a complete fool by not sharing any of this news with me. I'll feel like a stranger, an outsider. What will I say to people when they ask me about the company, about him? "Well, I have no idea, I haven't talked to the guy in seven years before last night." This is so not like the Charlie I knew, once, all those years ago. He would have asked me first, asked my permission even. We would have talked about it. He couldn't call me to share the news about the vaccine? Why keep me in the dark like this? It's hurtful.

I drag the wardrobe back to my room. I'm on edge and deflated. I try Mom a couple more times. No answer. It's clear she's turned her phone off. She must have stopped at church after the salon. She turns her phone off at church and frequently forgets to turn it back on again.

I need to talk to Charlie *Charles*. No, he needs to talk to *me*, more like it. He owes me a mile-long explanation. Until then, he's on my shit list.

I lay in bed with my robe on stewing for what seems like hours. It's 6:30. I'm resolved to stay home tonight. This is *his* show. My Mom's show. They can enjoy it. Revel in my Dad's success. I wasn't included, wasn't consulted or even told about it until last week. They don't need me.

I notice the door to Dad's old lab is still ajar and wander down the stairs. The back wall is packed from end to end with old filing cabinets. Every drawer is a different topic, an idea he had that either did or didn't come to fruition, his life's work. My Mom organized it all for him, racing against time to finish the massive task before he completely lost his memory. We should digitize it all. All this paper here in the basement doesn't make sense. I notice a drawer at the end of the row is partially open, a file hanging out. I walk over to tuck it back in and close the drawer but stop short when I notice the title: Earth Vision Concept. The file is old. I peek inside and the mathematical calculations and scientific notations are all written in pencil on graph paper that appears coffee stained. The date on the top corner of each page is February 7, 1989. Wow, that's quite a bit of time from concept to market. Geez, the guy was brilliant. He was truly brilliant.

Shit, I need to be there tonight. I need to be there for my Dad, to honor him. I need to press pause on this anger, this hurt I feel over the Charlie *Charles* revelation for this one night. Can I do it? I think so. I would do anything for my Dad. I shut the file drawer and reach down to tighten the tie on my robe. Shit, I'm still in a robe. Haven't done my hair. It's 6:45. I can make it. I'll just be a bit late. That's better anyway. I don't think I could handle *mingling* with the level of angst I feel toward a certain person right now.

On my way up the stairs I hear my phone buzzing. Three missed calls from a number I don't recognize. I ignore it. If it's *Charles*, or anyone associated with Mayvin, I don't want to talk to them. Just as I finish that thought my phone rings again. The same number. Oh, what the heck. I put it on speaker and listen for who's on the other end. "Ms. Mayvin?" "Yes, speaking." "It's Tom, your driver. I'm out front when you're ready." "Oh. I'm sorry, I completely forgot. Umm, I may be a few minutes. Can you wait?" "I've got all night Ma'am. Just come out when you're ready." "Thanks Tom." I reply and rush to open the wardrobe bag.

I'm secretly curious what Ms. Price picked out for this lover of classics with a touch of freckles and muscle tone. Geez Charlie, you might as well have told her I was a pudgeball in high school! I crack a sarcastic smile, making a mental note to call him out on his creepiness and shove that email in his face when the time is right. But I'm quickly distracted by the sight of two sets of hangers fastened together at the hook adorned with the most exquisite gowns I've ever seen – one navy blue and one a shimmering dark green. Both are simple and elegant and *very much* my style. Way to go Danika! Or should I say, Price. The navy blue is off-the-shoulder and cut-in slightly around the chest. It's tailored and sophisticated. The dark green gown is pleated tulle with a silk bodice underneath, A-line with a bateau neck and capped sleeves. Very Jackie O. Very my Dad. Very me. He loved when I wore green too. It's perfect. I peek in the bag and find a pearl-studded hair claw and dark green silk open-toed heels by some Italian designer whose name is on the insole. Nicely done, Price. I can do up-dos. I've mastered the art of up-dos and buns. Being a runner, I never have time to style my unruly hair.

I begin to slip on the dress in front of the closet mirror, thinking I should really hurry for Tom's sake. As I bring the bodice up to my chest, I notice a mark on my breast. A red and purple mark. A hickey-like mark. I look closer. Wait, it *is* a hickey. What?! No way. I haven't *been* with anyone. It's not possible. I must have scrubbed too hard in the shower. I continue to dress but then something stops me and I take another look in the mirror. It couldn't be. My mind takes me back to the dream last night. I mentally scroll through every detail. I dreamt his mouth was on me, there, where the mark is, and in other places too *lots of other places*. But it's not possible. I was dreaming. I resolve to put it out of my mind. This day just couldn't get any weirder. I hope to God dead people can't see what is happening on earth. I blush. My Dad would be so disappointed in me right now. If he knew ... and on the night of his funeral no less. I'm going to hell. That's for sure!

My phone rings. It's Pierce. I put him on speaker while I finish my makeup. "Hey, you? Coming tonight, right?" "Of course." I respond in my most dramatic sarcastic tone. "Doesn't sound very convincing. Listen, I'm sorry I haven't reached out. Mayvin's legal department is slammed right now. How was the funeral? Sorry I missed it." I can hear lots of loud mingling in the background. *Thank God I'm not there yet.* "I can imagine. Umm, it was a funeral.

Not something I was looking forward to, but, surprisingly ... healing."

"Good, you need to heal. Listen, you better get here soon. Cocktail hour is in full swing and Charles looks like he's about to lose it if you don't show."

"Oh, does he now? Well Charles can shove *it* up his ass."

"Yikes. What brought this on? Tuck your claws in, tiger. The guy just made you a ton of money and he's throwing a huge party in your Dad's honor. Cat, the *Vice President* is here!"

A lump forms in my throat. "I just don't like being kept in the dark, or coddled. I'm sure I'll get over it. Well, if the *Vice President* is there, I guess I better be on my best behavior. Do me a favor, ask him where the fuck Curt is!"

"Cat, seriously. He pauses. "Have you been drinking already?" He chastises me.

"Seriously? You're at a cocktail hour. One G&T, Pierce. I need to be on equal playing field with my *mingling* opponents."

"It's not a battle, Cat. It's a party. You know ... Hi, how are you? Where are you from? So good to see you again." He snides back.

"Yeah, well, some people do social better than I do. Listen, I'm just about on my way. If anyone asks, tell them not to hold up anything. I'll be there."

"See ya soon. And Cat, save a dance for me?"

I groan. "There's dancing? Seriously?" I complain.

"Cat, it's a gala. Also, apparently your parents loved to dance. Is that true?"

Huh?! "It is actually. Okay, one dance. Pierce, go. Mingle. I need to finish putting on my fake "glow" and Tom The Driver's waiting."

I make it out the door by 7:15 and Tom is leaning against the

Town Car waiting for me. I notice he's talking to someone in his earpiece as I approach and then abruptly ends the call. Perfect timing. With any luck, I'll arrive just as the cocktail hour is ending and I can slip in undetected, no spotlight on me.

13. CATHERINE

Tom stops the car in the middle of Constitution Avenue. The street is deserted save for a swarm of men who look like secret service. Shit, they probably are secret service. Tom has scooped me out of my seat and is waving me goodbye by the time I become aware I'm being patted down, clutch confiscated and ID scanned. A very handsome rock of a man with sunglasses and an earpiece leads me up the steps of the Smithsonian Museum of Natural History. The doors open for us by more crewmen and I'm in awe standing in front of the massive iconic elephant lit by evening string lights draped across the entrance hall. What a venue! What would my Dad think? At first, I see no one and can hear only whispers from what sounds like a crowd. Then, the crowd begins to appear as we move further into the impressive open space and I hear the sound of a woman's voice from a stage block at the far end of the room.

"My esteemed colleague *and boss*, the second CEO in Mayvin history, Mr. Charles H. Draper!" Applause erupt around the room and I take this as my opportunity to steal away and grab a spot behind a perimeter column to watch. But before I can settle on my intended hiding place, a tall, shaggy-haired blonde in jeans and a black button-down approaches me head-on. "Catherine. Welcome." He whispers in my ear with a dreamy Australian accent. "I'm Rorey, Head of Security for Mayvin. So glad you could make it. Follow me." He hooks his arm through mine as I smile back at him, shy and dumbfounded. He leads me to a break in the center of the crowd lined up for a direct view of the podium, the massive elephant behind me. I'm by myself, the crowd parted between me. Before I can notice he's gone, I'm staring at the stage and Charles is front and center before me, more gorgeous than he was last night. His dark unruly hair now slicked back to the side. His slightly tanned skin is glowing in the spotlights and his piercing brown eyes are fixed directly on me. He smiles shyly in my direction, his eyes now firmly fixed on mine and mine on his. If it's a staring contest, I'm losing. Where did my anger go? Then he begins to address the crowd.

Ladies and Gentlemen. Mr. Vice President. Prime Minister. Director Dorsey. Director Sparks. Dean Hirschman. Dean George. Professor Galloway. Mrs. Mayvin. Ms. Catherine Mayvin.

His voice is rich, smooth and mesmerizing. He's managed to draw the crowd in and he's only at introductions. With his last address, he lingers on my name and I go crimson. His eyes are, again, fixed on mine like lasers. I break eye contact and look around the crowd, still applauding but who have now all turned to stare in my direction. Oh God, did he have to address me? I glance up at him again, this time my eyes pleading with him to move on with his speech, the attention is too much to bear. He remains fixed on me still and I am left paralyzed, again pinned by his stare. He's a heady sight, a lot to take in. He trails a path with his eyes down to my toes and back up again then tilts his head and gives me a wink and a knowing smile as goosebumps light up my flesh. We remain like this for too long, until the hall is silent again save for a few whispers. Finally, he begins again.

Thank you for being here tonight to honor a great man. Dr. Blanton H. Mayvin, Jr was a scientist, a discoverer and searcher of truth. He never sought fame or glory, just results and solutions. Each idea or invention he pursued was rooted in hard science, conjured from his love of nature and his curious mind. His catalyst, an undying need to help save humankind from unnecessary peril or lack of technology. He believed there was a solution to every problem, a better way to every path we take. His curious mind - he shared with me one night in his laboratory when I was just 18 - was fueled by his love of nature and all things living and breathing. "We can learn so much from the creatures and plants and organisms around us." he told me. They are God's creations, complex perfect machines working around us; we should watch and learn from them. If we are to advance as a species, he said, we must learn from them. The reason we are standing here tonight in this grand hall, surrounded by impressive specimens of nature, is a tribute to Dr. Mayvin and his curious mind. It's a reminder to us all to never look past the wonder and complexity of the living resources around us, the ones we were born into this world with. Dr. Mayvin found his answers in the universe that exists around us now, today. So can we. It was Dr. Mayvin's lifelong dedication to learning and curiosity that literally saved the human race.

The crowd is now awestruck, sucking in a deep breath in unison across the room. Charles pauses for a moment. I search the room, tears clouding my vision, and finally notice my mother, to the right of the stage, patting a tissue against her face.

Tucked away in his basement laboratory freezer for the last five years, sat the results of one of Dr. Mayvin's pet projects – a cure for the common cold. It took weeks for us to uncover the gem hidden before us. His approach was unprecedented. Not surprisingly, rooted in the basic elements of cellular biology. The result was a vaccine that not only cured the common cold, but completely eliminates the entire strain of coronaviruses.

The crowd roars to life at Charles's shocking revelation. The grand hall sounds like an NFL football stadium after a game winning touchdown. I almost forget to join in, I'm stunned too by this announcement. My father discovered the cure to the pandemic virus of the 21st century, before the virus even came about! Charlie's right. He's a genius. Tears begin to fall and I'm suddenly unable to clap. I just wish I could see him one more time. Before I can begin weeping, Charlie *Charles* begins again.

And, as if that was not enough,

He yells over the crowd.

As if that was not enough, he introduced a novel approach to virus development that has the entire biomedical industry in a tailspin - the answer was so plain and simple - it was literally right in front of their noses for decades. Dr. Mayvin's genius knew no bounds because of his insatiable curiosity and his awestruck reverence of nature.

It is the greatest honor of my life to have had him as my mentor. He came into my life at a time when I needed him most. My father had disappeared and my mother had just passed away from cancer. He took me under his wing becoming the father I needed and the teacher I craved. He gave me the courage to follow my dreams and set the example to remain steadfast in my own search for truth. Every success Mayvin has seen since its inception, including our recent scientific breakthroughs, can be attributed to Dr. Mayvin and his lifelong pursuit of knowledge. You see, Dr. Mayvin grew up without a father too. Like me, he attributed his success in life to the kindness, support and guidance of one special person, his mentor, Dean Nigel George of Oxford.

Charles steps to the edge of the stage with the microphone and gestures toward Dean George, who is standing next to my Mom, calling him out to the crowd. The entire room erupts with applause for several minutes before Charles starts again.

Ladies and Gentleman, I have a special treat for you this evening, a video tribute to Dr. Mayvin, with footage from his years at Oxford, the early years of Mayvin Enterprises and the, now infamous, basement laboratory. The video will also introduce you to the foundation established in his honor; a foundation for youth around the country in need of a mentor and positive role models in their lives. Mayvin Enterprises has donated $5 million dollars *to start the R.H. Mayvin Foundation and in less than two months since its inception, over 250 mentors, leaders and professionals from all over the country, have pledged their support as a Mayvin Mentor. On behalf of Mayvin Enterprises and the R.H, Mayvin foundation, I would like to thank each of you for being here this evening to celebrate this special man and support this great cause so dear to his heart. But before we launch the video, I have two more individuals to recognize.*

First, I would like to recognize Dr. Mayvin's wife, Celia. Celia's un-wavering devotion and belief in her husband and all that he stood for is something I've witnessed firsthand over the years. Ladies and Gentlemen, when true love finds you, hold on to it, because I can tell you, from what I've seen, it can move mountains. Mrs. Mayvin and her love of her husband most certainly led this man to greatness.

Charles steps down from the stage, takes my mother's hand, kisses it and then presents her to the room for another round of applause from the crowd. I'm so awestruck by his entire per-formance by this point I am lost beyond any specific emotion. He knows my parents so intimately. I had no idea my Dad had a mentor from Oxford. I barely even remember my Dad studied at Oxford. And he and my Mom seem so familiar, so close. When did this happen? I feel like a stranger in the room.

Finally, Ladies and Gentlemen, there is one more person in the room this evening that I'd like to recognize. And it's important I recognize her because if it were not for her pure heart, her sincer-ity and true kindness, I would not be standing before you today. I came to live with my aunt one week after my mother died of cancer and 3 years after my father left for good, never to be heard from again. I had no friends. I was a lost soul. Catherine Mayvin was my aunt's closest neighbor. She saw me sitting alone on the bus, alone in the lunchroom, alone during recess and alone again on my walk home that afternoon. She only let that pass for one day before she approached me and asked me to be her friend. That one act of kindness began a chain reaction that led me to where I am today. Catherine, for your kind heart, thank you.

Charlie's *Charles's* words have transported me back to memories I've forgotten. Sweet memories from my youth walking down the rail path with Charlie to and from school. The first day I introduced him to Dad and we finished our earth science project together in the basement. I miss those days. I miss the friendship we had. I miss my Dad. I had no idea Charlie was so lost at the time. I knew his Mom had died but never knew about his father disappearing or what had happened. I thought he never even knew his father. Tears are streaming down my face now but before I can completely lose it, Charlie is standing next to me holding my hand out as the crowd begins applauding once again. Did he have to do this? I am so embarrassed and this night is so not about me. As I finish this thought, the video begins to play and the crowd finally settles down taking their eyes off of me. Charlie doesn't remove his hand from mine but instead positions himself behind me, bringing his other hand to settle on my waist and our clasped hands down at my other side. He leans in to whisper in my ear as a black and white image of my father materializes on the screen and the narrator begins. I look around to see if anyone is watching our intimate moment but the crowd appears engrossed in the film. *Thank God.*

"I hope you didn't mind that last part. I know how much you hate the spotlight. But it's something I've been meaning to tell you for a long time. Really, thank you. You saved my life that year Catherine, you really did. I don't think I would have been a normal kid if I hadn't had your friendship." His whispered voice is soft and sincere, tickling at my neck and sending shivers down my side. I turn to my side and look up into his eyes. Those familiar eyes, warm and welcoming, framed by such a gorgeous face I barely recognize but that every inch of me responds to nonetheless. "I had no idea." I reply, barely able to keep eye contact with him save for swooning right here and now. "It was nothing, really. You were as much my savior as I was yours." I continue, now staring at his gorgeous lips to avoid his eyes. Not any better. Why am I so affected by him? What has come over me? I'm supposed to be fuming at this guy who has literally taken over my family and my future inheritance without even a word to me in seven years. And yet, with his speech and the sincerity and the grand gesture of this entire evening and the foundation and just, him in general, I'm finding it very hard to be mad.

He leans in again, squeezing his hand tighter around my waist and bringing our clasped hands around us. I'm suddenly so light-headed, a breathless feeling comes over me. Seriously, Catherine, what is this? The 1790s? I'm literally swooning. Swooning over my high school best friend at my father's memorial. This is so out-of-body. He senses my sudden lack of stability and presses himself closer to support me as he whispers "I'll let you watch the video but I just have to tell you, once again, you take my breath away. You look absolutely stunning in that dress." At his mention of the dress I'm reminded of Danika Price and the email, of everything I've learned in the last two hours. Anger takes over my emotions, quelling the trail of goosebumps that had formed up and down my body from his attentions. I stiffen and he takes the hint, righting me and removing his hands from my waistline but keeping our right hands clasped. I remove my hand from his and tug down on his wrist turning my head and shooting him a look. "We need to talk." I spit out a little more harshly than I had intended. His eyebrows shoot up in reply and the man next to us turns his head. But Charlie's initial surprise quickly morphs into a knowing look. "I know." He replies this time in a less seductive, louder whisper. "We will, okay? After tonight, I promise." I let go of his wrist and fold my arms together, turning back to try and watch the video and ignore him. But I can't concentrate. All I see is red. He's still behind me. I can't miss his presence.

I turn back around and eye him again. Jesus, who molded this man? The sight of him in a tuxedo is a sight to behold. "When were you planning to tell me *Charles*?" I practically shout, emphasis on his newly adopted name. Shit, that was way too loud. I'm glaring at him now, my arms still folded in front of me. More heads turn in our direction and it's clear I've made a scene. His eyes first plead with me and then like a switch turned on, he grabs my arm and pulls me behind the columns, past the elephant and across the darkened side of the main hallway in one swift movement.

14. CHARLES

Things are very quickly heading in the wrong direction. What was I thinking, waiting until tonight for a big reveal? What had seemed like the right thing to do, waiting to tell her until the other situations in her life were settled, now suddenly seems so obviously a very wrong decision. She arrived way too late. Something delayed her. She knew before she arrived. I bet she almost didn't make it tonight. I'll set it right. Apologize. She'll hear it all from me in time. I just hope I can settle her anger to get us through the evening without a scene. She's pissed. Maybe I came on too strong. Shit, Draper, you did come on too strong. One look at her and I was toast. Lost in her eyes, her face, her skin, her hair, her gorgeous body in that dress. I can't help myself. It's hard to separate my two worlds with her. My psyche is drawn to her. I feel her struggling for release from my grip. Damnit Draper, this possessive shit has got to stop. I'm like a fucking ape-man around her. I gingerly swing her toward me catching my hand on the small of her back now guiding her toward the VIP room we set aside for the Vice President. She feels so right in my arms, it's like I know every inch of her body from memory. And I do.

Syd catches my eye as I lead her into the room. He nods as he approaches and shoots me an understanding look before shutting the door behind us. Catherine immediately storms several feet away from me before swiveling on point to face me, arms folded, her gown swishing abruptly in her wake as if to put an explanation point on her fervor.

"When were you going to tell me, Charlie? Huh? *Charles Draper*? I feel like I don't even know you anymore. You changed your name. You changed your, your … everything about you has changed!" She yells at me frantically. *Change is an understatement. What you've seen is only the tip of the iceberg, honey.* Holy Mother-of-All-Things, I want to take her in my arms and suck on that luscious bottom lip of hers right about now. Angry, on *her*, is irresistible. Shit, I've got to deal with this.

"Catherine, I'm sorry. I changed my name when I returned from my trip abroad. That journey changed … transformed me. I had some experiences and, well, I'm a new person. Draper was my father's name. I was born with his name but when he left, my mother changed it to her family name, Hearst, in anger, to forget him and out of spite. Charles is just who I am now, the boy I was is gone."

"I see…" She starts to respond and I can tell my explanation sobers her for a second and she stalls. "… But, I'm not referring to just that. You are the CEO of Mayvin now and you run this company and you *bought* the company and you didn't even tell me. You don't even talk to me, Charlie! We haven't really talked in seven years. My Dad was not well. How did this all come about? Did he just *give* you the company? Did you just *take* it? Why didn't you tell me about any of this?! Why am I l the last one to know?!" She's full-on frantic now and her accusations set me back. Oh Catherine, no, don't go there.

"Catherine, no! No, no, no. I would never. Catherine, when I came back from my trip, your father was in a bad way. I came back to my former position as a researcher, but it quickly became clear things were not going well with the company. I visited your parents every night, worried about your Dad. I was going to call you but then I heard about the wedding and the baby and everything after and I knew you had enough on your plate. *I couldn't bear to see you with another man.* It became clear the company was about to go under and I wanted to help. Your Dad was not well and your Mom was, well, Catherine, she was beside herself at his decline. Your Dad had so many near breakthroughs and I had an idea to make one of his technologies actually work. I had just inherited the house and land from my trust so I collateralized everything in my name and infused the company with cash. I only intended to purchase a small share of stock, just enough so I could complete the transaction and save the company from bankruptcy. Your parents insisted on offering me more. And, after the mess I'd un-covered during your Dad's decline, I was the only one he'd trust to lead the company. He insisted I take his place. None of this was for my own gain. Catherine, I did it all for your family ... for your Dad ... for you."

She's staring at me with a look of disbelief on her face, her cheeks still flushed with anger and wisps of orange and blonde hair fall-ing out of place. She's a gorgeous sight to behold. It's all I can do to restrain myself from rushing to her, gathering her in my arms and trailing kisses down her neckline to make her see the truth. She looks down for a moment, processing something, and then sud-denly her head shoots up, her eyes pinning *me* in place this time.

"When were you planning on telling me all of this Charlie? *Charles?* Was it seriously your plan to wait until tonight?!" She spits out incredulously.

She has me there. "In hindsight..."

She smells my blood in the water. "Yeah, in hindsight, dumb move *Hears ... Draper*. I don't even know what to call you anymore! How *dare* you decide what I should and shouldn't know about my own family! And my Mother! Were you behind her silence, or should I say, duplicitous references to *the new CEO*?"

Despite my verbal spanking, I meet her stare blink for blink try-ing to get her to calm down and really see me, to remember who she's talking to. I proceed calmly.

"Catherine, please don't be angry at your Mom. She was under the impression I was going to tell you at some point, before today. I asked her to wait until I could talk to you personally. This is my fault. Please don't bring her into this." I pause and wait for her to argue but she doesn't. "I'm curious, though. How did you find out? Earlier?"

"Price." She replies with a smirk. I cock my head at her, not understanding her reply at first. "You know? Danika, your wardrobe consultant? She left a print out of your email exchange in the hanging bag. Informative, eye-opening email, *Charles*." I slowly begin to close the distance between us, recounting every detail of that email in my mind as we continue our staring contest.

I'm so close to her now I can practically hear her heartbeat thudding under the emerald bodice. Her breathing is quick and heavy as if something intense is affecting her pulse. "Catherine, I'll always be Charlie for you." I whisper, staring deep into those gorgeous green eyes. She steps back as her checks turn crimson, her hand suddenly flies to her chest and she draws a breath in surprise."

"Catherine, what is it? What happened?"

"I just ... remembered something." Then her eyes go wide as if at some realization in her mind. "Did you? ... were you? No. Never mind."

"Catherine, what is it? Say it?" I plead with her in a whisper.

"Did you come back to my house last night?" *Oh!*

"Why do you ask?" *Don't be coy, Draper. Tell her.*

"Something happened and it's not possible ... it doesn't make sense..." I cut her off.

"Catherine, there's something else, something important I need to tell you about me and about ... us." I whisper at her lips.

"*Us*?!" She's surprised. "Charlie, there is no *us*." *Is she serious?*

"Catherine, there's so much *us* in the air I can reach out and grab it." Catherine falters and I catch her with my palm against her back before her legs give way. Her head leans back and her lashes are drawn, inviting me. Not able to resist the urge, I lean in to kiss her just as I hear the door fly open behind me. *Damn it, Draper, could you screw this up anymore?* Catherine rights herself at the sound of the door opening and attempts to peer around me yet I manage to hold her eyes in my direction. Syd clears his throat and addresses me from the doorway. "Chuck, sorry to interrupt, but the Vice President needs to leave and wants a word with you first. Also, Mrs. Mayvin is looking for Catherine."

"Perfect timing. Catherine, this is Rorey McCleary, Head of Security at Mayvin." "We've met." Syd replies from the doorway.

"Syd, Catherine has inquired about the security of her residence last night. Can you assure her she was alone in her home all evening after I left?" I ask.

"Catherine, my team is running 24-hour surveillance on your residence. After Chuck swept your house, no one entered or exited until you left for your run this morning. Chuck, the Veep's waiting."

Syd's right. I need to get this night back on track. I straighten my tie and attempt to close things with Catherine, for now, taking her chin in my hand. "As I said before, there is much more I need to explain to you about Curt, the security, me and last night." At the mention of *last night* her eyes go wide and cheeks blush again. "Care to join me and meet the Vice President?" She shakes her head in a vehement "No". "You should go see your Mom. Dinner's about to start. Save a dance for me." I wink at her and turn to leave the room. *God, I wish I knew what was in her head right now.*

15. CATHERINE

The intensity of our emotions is hanging in the air like a thick cloud of lust and butterflies are still swarming in my core. I've got to get out of this room before I combust. AHHH! The way my body reacts to him is infuriating. My brain completely shuts down. That was not how our exchange of words was supposed to go down. I had intended to berate him for his actions, until he walked away with his tail between his legs. Instead, he managed to seduce me to the point of swooning with one look in his eyes. I need a drink.

I attempt to put my hair back into place as I skulk out of the room not yet sure how to react to my Mother. As I make my way out in to the hall again, I run smack into her. "Oh, Catherine, come here!" She pulls me into her arms and then draws me out again to look at me. "You look stunning, absolutely stunning! Charles did well. He knows your style, doesn't he?" "Mom, *you* look gorgeous!" I attempt to change the subject away from a certain someone. And she does look amazing. She's wearing a light grey one-shoulder draped gown that shimmers in the light. Her hair is wisped to the side in the back. She could be a model. Seriously. She's perfection. "Wasn't that all so touching? Charles's speech?! The video?! Your father would be so proud, Catherine. Don't you think?" "Truly Mom, truly. He would." She smiles at me, questioning something in my mood with the tilt of her head. "Listen Mom, I got here late and I'm sure you're aware, but maybe not, I didn't actually know that Charles was *Charlie*. I'm just a bit taken back and I just want to grab a drink and take a minute. Okay?" "Catherine, I don't know what to say. I wanted to tell you but he insisted on telling you directly. I assumed he had told you when you came back this winter before Dad passed. It was only the other day he confessed to me he actually hadn't seen you *nor* talked to you. I found it hard to be mad at him, Catherine. After all he's done. Please don't be upset." "Mom, I'm not upset with you. Okay, I'm upset, but I'll get over it. I just need a few minutes, okay?" "Of course. I'll cover for you in the meantime, but don't take too long. There is a sea of people *dying* to meet you, honey." *Yeah, well, I'll take a rain check.*

I scan the room and spot a bar counter set up on the outskirts of the room with no line. Nodding affirmatively to my Mom, I squeeze her hand and make my way over to the oasis grabbing a pre-poured glass of champagne from the counter. I'm seconds away from my intended hiding spot, a dark row of columns ahead of me, when I feel a hand on my shoulder. "Cat! Where have you been hiding?" Shit, it's Pierce! I really don't need this right now. Before turning around to face him, I down the champagne in one gulp. Desperate times. Desperate Measures. "Hi." He says when I'm facing him. "Hi Pierce!" I do my best to fake an I'm-so-happy-to-see-you face for the friend who's been so good to me the last several months. "You look absolutely stunning, Catherine. God girl, you really do clean up nice!" He says so sincerely to me as he grabs my free hand. I can't help but smile. "Thank you. You don't look too shabby yourself, kid. I bet you're turning heads with all the ladies tonight." Wow, something about seeing Pierce is making me feel normal again. "Yeah, right." He chides. "Hey, it looks like you need another drink. Champagne?" "Yes, please!" I reply, a little too enthusiastically, and he laughs. "You got it." No sooner does Pierce return with my champagne when bells begin to chime from the quartet in the center of the room, signaling dinner. Out of nowhere, Rorey *Syd* swoops in from behind to escort me to my table. *Where did he come from?* Pierce looks just as dumbfounded as me. "I'll come find you after dinner for that dance, okay? I'm being requested to sit with the legal team."

He waves goodbye as Rorey glides me to the front of the room near the stage where my mother and six other men are seated. Rorey slides one of the two remaining chairs out for me to take a seat. When he moves to tuck the chair in, I glance over and notice Charles's name on the tent card for the empty seat next to me. The man's got some balls. I have half a mind to smack him across the face when he finally makes it to his seat. For what, exactly, I think to myself. For not talking to me? For waiting this long to tell me about so many important details? For not being my friend all of these years? For making me long for him in my sleep? For making me swoon with desire in his presence? For moving me to tears tonight over his devotion to my father? For caring so deeply for my parents? For making me feel so ... what does he make me feel? The words *loved* and *cherished* pop into my head and I feel warm all over for a minute. But I let my anger take over again because deep down I know it's true, how he makes me feel, and I'm not yet ready to surrender to it and forgive him. Something in my gut tells me that the second I surrender and the dam breaks, I'll be faced with an ocean of feelings I'm not yet ready to face.

At that thought, I down the glass of red wine in front of me only to have it refilled immediately for my wallowing pleasure. I stare at the glass again, before taking another sip. Nope, not ready to deal with my feelings tonight. Bottom's up girl! "2016 Haut Brion." Booms a polished British accent into my left ear. I turn to my left and stare into the most inviting brown eyes of a very debonair older man with slicked-back white hair wearing a very expensive looking evening suit fitted with a plaid bowtie. He's channeling Sir Anthony Hopkins and it's working for him. "Excellent vintage." He continues. "Draper knows a good wine. That's a good quality in a man, you know? Probably learned it from Blanton. But then again, everything Blanton knew about wine, he learned from me." "Oh hi!" I shriek, finally recognizing who is talking to me. "You're Dr. George!" "Call me Nigel." He replies. "I'm Catherine, Blanton's daughter."

"Yes, I know, dear. I know who you are. Your father boasted about you every chance he could get. In our email exchanges over the years, he would go on and on about his talented, beautiful, intelligent daughter. And now that I see you in the flesh, I'd say his carrying-on was quite an understatement. You're stunning. Simply stunning. And you clearly know a good wine, so you've got a good head on your shoulders too. That's all a father could ask for." I laugh and he smiles back at me. We continue on like this all through dinner. He shares story after hilarious story about my father and about his life in the UK. He's a fantastic storyteller and I'm so engrossed, it doesn't hit me until my dinner plate is taken away that Charlie has yet to take his seat.

I scan the room a few times but see no signs of him. *Maybe he's hiding from me?* I glance across the table during the few breaks in our conversation and notice my mother similarly engrossed in a very intimate exchange with a man I recognize but can't quite place. By the time the dessert and coffee are being served, Nigel and I have downed two bottles of the Haut Brion Bordeaux. *Oh lord!* I better call this a night for alcohol. I haven't had this much to drink in one night since undergrad.

The band begins in full swing with *Girl from Ipanema* and Nigel stumbles to his feet, his nose a Rudolph red as he gestures for my hand. "May I?" Why not! For Daddy, I say to myself. "Why Nigel, I thought you'd never ask!" I tease. He lets out a loud bellow that warms my heart and leads me to the dance floor. We glide across the floor, I imagine like Gene and Fred. Nigel's got the moves! Nigel spins me in and out with surprising grace considering our state of inebriation. I look around the dance floor and notice, at first, my mom is dancing rather closely with the familiar gentleman from our table I still can't place. Another glance around the room and my eye catches on a tall, elegant woman with long, shiny dark hair in a tightfitting silver studded gown featuring a dramatic open back, the fabric pooling at her lower back. My eyes move to her dance partner's hand clutching her waist, his fingertips just touching the exposed skin of her back. I follow the hand up the arm to his shoulder and face. To my surprise, Charlie's head is bent over to be close to hers, a serious expression on his face. They're engaged in an intimate conversation, both heads nodding and animated in response to each other as he glides her across the dancefloor. She moves closer to him and his hand adjusts down her waist. I'm hit with a sudden pang of jealousy. *Who is that woman?* Why do you care, Catherine? You just told him to his face there is no *us*.

The music stops and Nigel leaves me with a dramatic bow. "Ladies and Gentleman, please return to your seats for a champagne toast in honor of our dear friend, Blanton." The gentleman with my mother announces, microphone in hand, his free arm draped around my mother's waist. Then it comes to me. He's Richard Downey, my parents' close friend. His wife died of cancer before I left for college. Hmmm. Something's definitely up between them. Great, just what I need, another drink. I head back to the table for the toast and down yet another glass of champagne. I'm now feeling a bit dizzy and find I'm being dragged to the dancefloor once again, this time by Pierce. It's a song I don't recognize, swing I think, still Pierce takes it as an excuse to wrap his arm almost completely around my back, pulling my chest toward him so we're sandwiched in an awkwardly close dancing embrace. "Pierce, there's plenty of room on this dancefloor." I motion between us. "I have more control this way. It's a swing dance, babe, and you're wasted. Can't have the guest of honor flailing about on the dancefloor." "I am so not wasted, Pierce. What makes you think that?" I laugh at him, my head falling back. I am *soooo* wasted. "Cat, come on. I watched you obliterate two $800 bottles of wine with that Brit friend of your Dad's." I bring my head back in place. What did he say?! "$800 a bottle! Are you serious, Pierce?!" "Umm, yeah. I looked it up. Your friend Charles has expensive taste." "He's not my friend." I reply hastily. "Oh, really?" He chuckles at me.

"Hey, Pierce?" I ask. "Who's that tall woman with the long dark hair that Charlie, I mean Charles, was dancing with?" "Oh, you don't know her? That's Caroline Benson. She's Lead Counsel for Mayvin. She's my boss. *Oh.* She and Charlie are really close. They've been spending a lot of time together working through the vaccine logistics. *Double Oh.* I think you'd really like her, Cat." *Fat chance on that, Pierce.*

16. CHARLES

This night is definitely not going as planned. I've been on edge since cocktail hour when Catherine failed to show. The only part that managed to go well was my introduction, not surprisingly the only part I could fully control. After I left Catherine, the Vice President waylaid me with news from Syria. A Special Ops force on the ground believe they've located Curt and two others from his mission. He's asked Syd and I to join their videoconference at midnight to confirm their rescue strategy. And, apparently POTUS isn't thrilled with the recent bent the media is taking on the vaccine release. Our media relations team is releasing way too many details to the press. Not sure if I agree. Isn't transparency what the public needs right now? By the time he finished with me, dinner was over and the dance floor in full swing, my plans to spend the evening with Catherine now OBE. I search the dancefloor for her but I'm stopped in my tracks by Caroline tugging at my arm. She asks me to dance and, frankly, it's the last thing I want to do right now. I just want to find Catherine and be with her. Hold her. Dance with her. I need to share the news about Curt, too. She deserves to know.

Caroline's been sending signals that she's interested in me. I'm not biting but she won't take the hint. I resolve to put a stop to it once this first push with the vaccine is behind us. Considering I'll be engaged with the Syria call most of the night, I need to direct Caroline on the media strategy now, before tomorrow morning's call with the press. "Caroline, we need to chat for a minute." "Hello to you too, Charles. Subject?" "The press." I reply. "Chat while we dance?" She asks. I guess one dance won't hurt. Thirty seconds in and I immediately regret it. Caroline is arguing against POTUS's reaction, which I can't blame her for but can do nothing about, all the while adjusting herself so my hands keep sliding further onto her inappropriately bare back. This is a memorial dinner to honor a dead man, Caroline, not a NY fashion gala. I remove my hand from her back altogether but find she's taken the wrong message as I'm now touching her upper thigh. Christ. Finally, *Girl from Ipanema* ends and I manage to get her to accept the new position for tomorrow's press briefing without having to get too stern with her. I look up and locate Catherine, who's adorably accepting a parting bow from Nigel. The scoundrel. He better behave himself.

Richard starts his toast and I catch sight of Syd motioning for me once more. What now? Turns out Syd's gotten a read-ahead from his special ops friend about the intricacies and risks of the rescue attempt. The security where these jerks have Curt held hostage is pretty sophisticated. Syd and his friend have a preferred approach and want to make sure I'm aligned before the call tonight. I assure him I'm on board. He's got my full trust. These bastards are blackmailing Mayvin and threatening the security of a few key people in my life. *One in particular.* Syd can tell I'm itching to end our conversation. "Good. I'm glad we're aligned." I turn to walk away, eager to find Catherine. "Chuck, just one more thing." I glance back at him, exasperated. "She's just guzzled two bottles of the good stuff with Dr. Bowtie over there. Not to mention the champagne. I'd caution you to gauge her mental state before you share this news." *Shit.* Security's been sending me reports of Catherine's daily activities over the past several months, ever since the threats started, and I doubt she's got a tolerance for half that much. Syd's right. I should hold off telling her until we learn more from tonight's call.

I spot her immediately. Actually, I spot Pretty Boy *The Third* with his hands all over her backside. *Hands. Off.* Two long strides later and I'm across the dancefloor scooping her from his arms on a downswing. *That was easy.* Staring into those gorgeous green eyes again, "May I?", I ask. She blinks at me several times in awe of my surprise appearance, then slowly nods her consent. "I'll take it from here, Buchanan." *Mine.*

"Hi." She says in the sweetest, shyest tone, her eyes searching me for an answer to where I've been for the last two hours. "Hi yourself." I answer back, my eyes pleading with her to forgive me for everything, my temporary absence included. Then, as if the universe is on our wavelength, the band strikes up in full Sinatra glory with *Summer Wind.* A Doc Mayvin favorite. The energy between us is visible. Our fingers and palms pressed together, arms wrapped around each other, sending an electric current of sensations down my body. Every glimmer from her eyes into mine fuels my heat. It's intense. Does she feel it too? God, I hope so. I move my hand to the small of her back, searching her eyes for permission, and then gently begin stroking up and down. I want her to know how much I've longed for her and how much she means to me. I want everyone around us to disappear and spend the next week just touching every inch of her, making her mine. We're swaying on the dancefloor now, just barely though, transfixed by each other. Suddenly everything we've both endured up until this night seems now to have had a purpose. It led us here.

Out of nowhere, something shifts in her expression and she lifts her chin, guarded. "Did you get your fill of your dance partner?" She accuses me. She's jealous! I direct her chin back with my thumb so I can see her eyes again. "Why, Ms. Mayvin? I believe your eyes are greener." I tease, now stroking her cheek. She blushes and turns away, ignoring my comment. "That dance was business. We have a media call tomorrow and the President's not happy with the way Caroline's team is handling things." I try to read her face. She appears unconvinced but slightly pleased. "Which reminds me. Now that the cat's out of the bag, so to speak, I owe you a briefing on the state of the company. Whenever you require it, Madame Shareholder, we shall deliver. I assure you, all is in good hands. You have a phenomenal team at the helm." This gets her attention and her eyes are back with me. "No. It looks to me like Daddy made the right choice ... on his replacement." A lone tear streams down her face as her lips begin to quiver and my heart breaks. Instinctually, I grab her face in my hands and take her in an embrace. She buries her face in my chest and begins sobbing. *Oh Catherine, no. Don't cry.* Once again the band delivers with a soothing number and I envelop her in my arms. After several intimate minutes like this, I reach into my chest pocket and hand her the decorative silk to dry her face. It's all I have. She looks up and I take her face in my hands again. Her eyes gleaming at me. *I love you, Catherine Mayvin.*

"Catherine, dear! There's someone I'd like to reintroduce you to." We both turn to our left, as if waking from a dream, to find Mrs. Mayvin and Richard Downey standing next to us waiting for an invitation to chat. *Oh shit.* Catherine has no idea about these two, does she? Damnit Celia. Timing is everything. How am I half your age and you haven't learned this by now? I manage to carry Catherine through the reintroduction to Richard. She is beyond drunk at this point and neither her Mom or Richard can tell she's been crying. My arm is firmly around her, keeping her upright. Unfortunately, the entire company sees this as their moment to meet Ms. Catherine Mayvin, the *very drunk* woman of the hour, apparently. To her credit, supported by my side, she feigns sobriety incredibly well. Dazzling everyone I introduce her to with her quick wit. *That's my girl!* It's not until Caroline Benson makes her introductions that her claws and her drunken state present themselves. "Caroline! So good to meet you!" Catherine lays it on thick, grabbing Caroline's hand in the process, practically stumbling into her, face first, before I can catch her. Caroline hardly notices the mishap, unable to remove her attention from my arm draped around Catherine's waist. I catch Caroline's eye roll before she saunters off toward the exit. *That went well.*

I look up to find Syd's finger twirling in the air and he catches my eye. "Wrap it up, Chuck." He mouths. I check my watch. 11:30. *Shit.* We'll have to start the call from the car. At this very moment I'm thankful for Richard who is, fortunately for me, tracking my exchange with Syd. "I'll close up here, Charles. You go." I nod. "Thanks Richard. I owe you." "Not a chance." He replies.

Catherine looks up at me, her eyelids droopy. There's no way I'm sending her home alone tonight. Sorry kid. I'll apologize for this tomorrow. You're coming with me. I reach down and grab her legs from behind, lifting her into my arms. "You read my mind, Chuck." Syd calls from behind, following us out the door. "Tom's waiting for us at the entrance."

Catherine wraps her arms around me, settling her head on my chest. She sighs and whispers, just barely audible. "You feel like home." *Ditto, baby. Ditto.*

17. CHARLES

We're in the Lincoln speeding down I-66, Catherine is passed out, draped over my lap and nuzzled into my chest. I texted Melinda earlier with the latest news on her son so I'm not surprised when I hear the buzz of an incoming call through my AirPods. "Melinda." I answer. "Charles, listen, I'll be quick. I know you've got the call in 3 minutes. Just ... she sighs into the phone they need to know how reckless he can be. He comes from three generations of war heroes and that stuck with him. ROTC and the MBA were tame by comparison, and they were not Curt's speed, at all. He only went that path to please me. He will try to be the hero, Charles. He will sacrifice himself for the good of democracy. Frankly, I'm surprised it hasn't happened already. If he catches even a whiff of a compromise on our part, he'll throw himself in harm's way. That rescue team needs to know. Okay? Please tell them." Damn, she's a good mother. The most insightful woman I've ever met. I hang my head in despair at her pleading. Fuck! My actions started this shitstorm chain reaction and I'm helpless to fix it on my own. "I've got it Melinda. Read you loud and clear. Rest assured your message will be passed along." I assure her. "Thank you, Charles. Truly, thank you for everything." "Melinda. Mayvin and I are responsible for this mess, for your son's disappearance. Please don't thank me. We owe this to you and to Curt."

"Charles, it's late so I'm not gonna argue with you, but you and I know that's not how this went down. Curt made his bed with active duty. It's what he always wanted. Plain and simple. Before you go, though, tell me. Does she know?" "Catherine? No, not yet.

It's been a long night. I plan to fill her in first thing." She's quiet for several seconds. "Don't wait too long, Charles. She's been in the dark on all this for way too long. I know how you feel about her. Don't risk creating a rift between you, Charles. She deserves you. You're the good guy. Her knight in shining armor, but, if you keep on keepin' that poor girl in the dark she's gonna paint you as the bad guy in her head and that happily ever after story you're aiming for's gonna slip right through your fingers." Melinda's Tennessee accent thickens with the intensity of her tone. I swallow a lump in my throat hoping to God Melinda is not the Shakespearian soothsayer who's just predicted my inevitable downfall. "Melinda, no truer words have ever been spoken. My fate with her hangs in the balance. She made that very clear tonight. Starting tomorrow, I'm an open book with her. Full transparency. She will know about Curt and everything else I've left out. If my day of reckoning comes, though, and she wants nothing to do with me, I take some comfort that I have you as a very reputable witness to my good intentions?" "Of course! Silly boy. I love that girl way too much to let her ruin her chance at happiness. Now, go try to save my son from being the damn hero."

18. CATHERINE

I wake with that feeling like I'm not where I'm supposed to be. The covers feel thick, cool and sleek around me. A welcoming comfort to my furnace-like body, working overtime to rid itself of the last remnants of wine. A dull ache comes to life around my temples when I attempt to lift my head from a very luxurious canopy of pillows around my head. Flashes of last night begin to reveal themselves and I settle back down to the comforts of this bedding fantasy. I breathe in and inhale a very familiar scent. Charlie. My eyes pop open and I look around me. The bed is massive, larger than a king. It's empty save for me, the covers untouched except for the space I occupy. Phew! My dress is draped along the foot of the bed and I feel under the covers to assess my current attire. Bra, check. Panties, check. Please tell me I had enough wherewithal to undress myself last night? I try to think back to my last memory from the evening. I got nothing. Damnit. Catherine Victoria Mayvin. What on earth were you thinking?! I lay like this for a minute, cursing myself, willing the pulsating pressure in my forehead to cease. Leaning up on my elbows to get my bearings, the room is nothing but grey and stark whites. Grey walls. Driftwood colored furnishings trimmed in a dark grey steel. Modern but warm. White trim. White doors. White bedding. Contemporary. Stylish. Fresh. I like it. I recall Aria's comment about the house, "Don't judge me when you see it, Cat." I wonder if this is Charlie's taste or a decorator's? Hmm. I wonder if Mom shared her decorator with Charles? Or, maybe Price dabbles in interior decorating.

I sit up and scooch to the end of the bed. On the nightstand sits a glass of ice water and a bottle of Advil. Someone's been here recently. The ice is fresh. I down three Advil and chug the water, several drops escape and dribble down my chest. Way too cold. When I set the glass back down I notice a stack of books behind the lamp. The books are neatly displayed like a decorative addition except for the one laying on top, set awry and pried open by a marker. I lean in closer and read the gilded writing on the worn leather spine. *Jane Eyre.* He's reading Jane Eyre?! *A man after my own heart.* I wonder what page he's on? My subconscious kicks into high gear. *No Catherine, this is no good. You need to get dressed and hightail it out of here before you have to face "You Know Who" half naked with his Bronte book in your hands, no less!* Shit, I'm so right. Here I am stuck between doing the walk of shame in my parent's neighborhood and stumbling over my emotions and embarrassment with Mr. Confusing. I stall and opt for the bathroom as a good interim step. I scope out the room and then make a break for the bathroom door. Holy wow, and I thought *my* new bathroom was nice. This is over the top! White and grey marble from floor to ceiling. A massive pool fills the middle of the room. Is that supposed to be a bath tub? It takes me a few minutes to locate the toilets, two of them, each with their own door opposite each other. Expecting company Charlie? Oh! I wonder how many women he's brought here? A flashback of Charlie dancing with Pierce's boss pops into my head. I don't like it. I vaguely remember meeting her. Shit, what did I say to her? Peeking around the door to the sink I notice a stack of white towels and a folded white t-shirt. After washing my hands and face, I throw on the t-shirt and pad my way back to the bedroom hopeful I'm still alone. The room is not as massive as it felt before, paling in comparison to that mega-bathroom with the pool! Uncle Robert must have left Charlie a small fortune. Either that or Mayvin's *paying* him a small fortune. Well, he did offer to give me a company briefing. Would it be rude if I asked about his compensation package? I really should shut down this suspicion I keep harboring toward him. After all, this is Charlie we're talking about. It wasn't long ago, I would have trusted my life with him. He seemed genuinely in pain last night when I suggested he may have acted in any way other than in my family's best interest. I resolve to give him the benefit of the doubt from this point forward. I can't even imagine how he orchestrated the effort to uncover Dad's ten-year-old vaccine, not to mention the earth vision thing. I have a feeling I've only begun to scratch the surface of Charlie's impact on Mayvin.

I notice a door on the other side of the bathroom. It's slightly ajar and light is streaming through the doorway. Curiosity gets the better of me. I sneak over toward the door and glide it open slowly, feeling like a bit of a snoop. Peeking in, it's clearly an office – a massive office. Not quite as massive as the en suite bathroom, but it will do. A floor to ceiling window adorns the back wall, the woods fronting the CIA building in full view. An oversized distressed wood desk matching the bedroom furniture and lined with large computer monitors sits not far from the window. But it's the two walls on either side of the room lined with white boards that catch my attention. To my left, I'm drawn to a massive map of the middle east taped to the white board and a timeline of sorts drawn in marker with pictures taped under each date. I instinctively turn behind me to be sure I'm alone and tiptoe over to the board. Pictures of Curt and his team are lined along the left of the board in a column format. Next to them are headshots of Syrian rebels. The timeline is piecing together the last known whereabouts and movement of each individual on the left of the board. I scan the timeline which starts just before Curt's disappearance. Impatient, I jump to the end and find, to my surprise, Curt has been located at a hostage location in Syria 2 days ago. He's alive! I scan the timeline again for any other clues or hints or signs of him before the incident. Nothing but hunches and leads until two days ago.

Why did I not know about this? Has anyone told Melinda? What's the plan to rescue him? My blood begins to boil. I can feel it start in my gut and rise to my head, my heart racing with anger. Why am I always in the dark, Charlie?! Why do you know about this and not me? A box outlined in red marker toward the bottom of the board catches my eye with the words "Ultimatum" and "Credible Threat". I read the summary. Holy shit, my name is listed. Charles Draper and Rorey McCleary received a phone call from the purported leader of the Syrian force who claimed to have Curt hostage, threatening harm to him and to his wife, the owner of Mayvin Enterprises and Charles, himself, if they didn't immediately turn over the design specifications for Project EarthScope. Oh! So that's the reason for the security. Well, damn. He could have just told me. I'm suddenly paralyzed, a chill running through me. This is scary, really scary. How did we get their attention? What's so critical about this technology? I stare at the board in silent disbelief for several minutes, soaking in all the details. This is major. This is way over my head. Charlie owes me answers. Suddenly Melinda pops into my head. Melinda! Does she know? I need to talk to Melinda. My phone. Hopefully it's still in my clutch. I think I saw it on the edge of the bed under my gown. I run out of the room but an image on the far wall catches my eye. The image is of me, running on campus by the stadium. I stop dead in my tracks and scan the wall. Images of me running, leaving the grocery store, walking into my house, leaving my house, studying on the campus greens, walking with Pierce. It's creepy. Really creepy. What. The. Fuck. I make my way along the wall, picture after picture, an uneasy feeling building in my gut. What was the purpose of this? My safety is one thing, but my picture on display like this is taking it to a whole new level. It's just creepy. I end the horrifying wall-walk and land at the start of Charlie's massive desk. It's protected with a glass cover and pictures fill the entire surface. Pictures of me. Only this time they are actual pictures of me, from high school with Charlie, from college, with my parents. I look further and see a few pictures of Charlie on his epic trip on tops of mountains, on beaches, in jungles, with people he's met along the way. There's one 5x7 of Charlie with his arm around an old man with grey hair. He looks like he's in Asia, mountains in the background. I linger on the picture and wonder who the man is. His eyes look kind, they have depth. I step back and scan the desk and walls again with a rush of emotions flooding through me. My instincts tell me to get the hell out of here, fast. I need my head on straight before I confront Charlie about all this crazy. I want answers and explanations, but the thought of seeing Charlie right now. It wouldn't go well. My heart is racing, beating out of my chest. I try to commit this room to memory and resolve to leave, grab my purse, dress and run home.

That's when a door to my left comes into view. It's mostly open unveiling a beautifully crafted hardwood staircase leading to a lower floor. Shit. This must be where Charlie is. My damned curiosity takes over my instinct to flee and I'm peeking in the door and halfway down the stairs before I can check myself. My eyes adjust to the barely lit stairwell as I make my descent and a vast chamber of pale gray stamped concrete unearths itself before me. I peer over the stair railing to catch a better glimpse of the vast cylindrical chamber that continues for what appears to be miles below me, notched in an even circular pattern like a tunnel until it ends in a softly illuminated dark-grey concrete slab. What is this place? Some kind of test lab for EarthScope? Well, it's creepy Charlie. Don't build this kind of shit in your house, weirdo! At that thought, my mind suddenly flips to my Dad and his now-infamous basement laboratory. *How is it those two are so similar?*

As much as I am pretending to be creeped out by this surprise door basement abyss, there's something strangely comforting and almost womblike in the air around me down here. There's a faint buzzing sound all around me. It's a vibration of sorts. Constant. Soothing. I can't quite grasp what it is but the tension from the revelations of the last twenty minutes is quickly lifting and my instinct to flee is melting fast down here. I'm so mesmerized by the concrete below me, I almost miss the fact I've arrived at a stair landing. My foot slips on a piece of paper hanging off the edge of the last stair and I grab the railing to catch myself letting out a gasp that echoes through the vibrations in the air around me. I hold my mouth and search the area for any movement. With the landing before me there appears to be a new set of rooms and an open gym or workout room opening up to my right. I look down to see the paper flip over as it glides to the floor at the landing and my eyes fix on a color image of Curt dressed in uniform in the middle of the page.

Department of the Army, Special Operations Force

RESCUE MISSION REPORT, August 4th 2020

I skip the summary and fix on the disturbing word under Curt's name and photo.

CPT CURTIS STARNES
STATUS: DECEASED

Deceased. He's dead. I collapse like an accordion on the stairs. No! No, no, no! No! Oh God, no!

19. CHARLES

The entire night was a shit show. I've been on edge since I tucked Catherine into bed. Something didn't smell right to me about the rescue mission. Curt knew a lot more from the inside than the ranger team on the ground. That much is abundantly clear now, in hindsight. Hindsight. Hah. My fucking life story is hindsight. It's all playing out in my head now, over and over. Curt was brilliant. While we orchestrated the mission from the outside, he was steps ahead of us. He clearly predicted our flawed plan and when the rescue team's cover was blown, Curt came out of nowhere, throwing himself into the crossfire long enough for the three other hostages to escape and for Curt to seal his fate. Heroic. Selfless. The ultimate sacrifice. He calculated the odds and, to him, he won the battle sacrificing his own life for three others to walk free. I'm in awe. I've spent the last year loathing the guy, despising him for having what I wanted with Catherine and taking that for granted. For giving those assholes a reason to come after her. For making her suffer. For not being good enough for her. Or, so I thought. In the end, turns out, he's made of the very best stuff. If anyone was deserving of her, it would be Curt. How do I tell her? How do I explain to her that if it were not for me, he would be alive today?

I've spent the last hour on the phone with Melinda who, sage woman that she is, predicted this entire scenario and, as a result, is mentally in a much better place than my sorry self. She would lecture me if she heard me taking any blame for his death, but the truth is, I'm the ultimate cause. I set the chain in motion after all. She doesn't know the specifics, the details I intend to share with Catherine very soon, at my peril, no doubt, but she knows enough, that I did something unspeakable to throw Catherine into Curt's arms that night.

It's 7am and I'm a live wire. Nine miles on the treadmill has done nothing to slow my racing thoughts. I check in on Catherine and leave a glass of ice water and ibuprofen beside her on the night stand. Sitting beside her on the bed, I linger on her peaceful face. She's gorgeous. Her sun-kissed nose and cheeks sprinkled with pale freckles from her summer afternoon runs. I stroke her golden locks, moving them to reveal her delicate shoulders and neckline. I need to get the hell out of here. Fast. Before I'm tempted to devour her and wake her into this nightmare of a day. The irony is not lost on me that I finally have her here with me after all these years, yet she's still out of reach.

Alone with my thoughts and restless, I know the only thing for me at this point is meditation. I head back through the office and down the stairs, grabbing the one-pager of last night's mission off the printer on my way down the stairs. I read it over and over as I descend the staircase shaking my head in disbelief. Fucking. A. Curt managed to save three of his men and assassinate a whole house full of Syrians in his grand finale departure from this world. Not too many men in history that measure up. Fatigue from the sleepless night is setting in and I let the page slip through my fingers and fall to the ground as I make my way below. How will I tell her? I always knew once I told her the odds of her wanting anything to do with me were slim to none. But now, after what I did caused Curt's death, she will never speak to me again. These thoughts remain with me as I turn on the steam shower in the meditation chamber. Twenty minutes later, I'm now wet, still on edge and dog tired. I shrug it off and take my position on the meditation slab. This time is different. Catherine is fast asleep, safe in my room so my subconscious leaves her be. *A first*; it's got one place to go, one person to get itself right with at the moment. Clouds, mountains, rivers, streams and lowlands morph into oceans and then inlets and then mountains again and finally sand unfolds for miles. And then there appears before me the spirit of the man I have loathed these fifteen long months. The man who was in the wrong place at the very wrong time and took her from me, took the possibility of *us* from me. And he's smiling. The son-of-a-bitch is smiling at me.

20. CHARLES

Vrrb, vrrb. Vrrb, vrrb. The buzzing makes its way to my consciousness as if I'm waking from a dream. I'm coming out of a deep state that keeps drawing me in, the serenity of his presence with me is enlightening. A level of awareness I've barely approached in the past. Who knew there were levels beyond what I'd already achieved. It's amazing. I want to share this with Catherine one day, to let her know it's all been for a purpose. Maybe I could bring her with me to see him. Vrrb, vrrb. Vrrb, vrrb. The buzzing begins to control my thoughts and my consciousness takes over, restarting my human senses. My eyes dart open and I can immediately tell by the shifting of the shadows in the chamber that it's late morning. Shit! I jump from the slab and head to the source of the buzzing. My phone. It's Syd. I answer it.

"Chuck?" "Yes." I respond in a hoarse tone I wasn't expecting. "Thank. Fuck. You're finally back to the land of the living. I was about to head down there myself and shake you." "Syd, what time is it?" "Chuck, listen. You need to stay calm. It's 11am." "Fuck!" I start to run upstairs with the phone still on speaker. "Chuck, stop right there." Syd calls from the upper landing. We meet each other half way and I motion to shove past him but he shoves me back. "Listen, asshole. I've been calling you for the past 30 minutes. I was this close to waking your fucking nirvana-ass up, okay? This fucking close! We had no surveillance on her in your room, Chuck. Your orders. We assumed she was safe. Asleep. The alarm went off in the garage over an hour ago. I was out. Backup investigated and found the Model 3 missing. We put the house on lockdown and searched your room. Chuck, she's gone." "She's gone?" I repeat, again hoarse, my disbelief barely audible. Syd shakes his head. I push him out of the way and he doesn't fight me. I take the stairs two at a time back through my office and then deliberately slow myself down as I enter the bedroom. I scan the room and reality sets in when I see the empty bed. Her emerald gown is still draped at the edge of the bed where I left it along with the matching clutch. A familiar piece of paper is crumpled on top of the dress, Curt's now distorted picture and knowing half smile staring back at me. Mocking me.

I hang my head in disbelief. This is my worst nightmare. She knows. She knows all the wrong information. How could I be so careless? I need to find her and explain. Seal my fate. She will never forgive me for what I've done.

Syd begins in a soothing monotone behind me. "We searched the house. She's been gone for hours now." My eyes go wide with fear. "It's not what you think, Chuck. She's okay. She stole your Tesla. We believe she's on her way to Tennessee." *Melinda. Of course she'd go directly to Melinda. She probably thinks Melinda has no clue.* "Chuck, the threat is gone now. Curt made sure of that last night. She's safe."

As if that were any consolation. For the second time since I first laid eyes on her, I'm certain there is no hope of ever having her in my arms again. Quite possibly never having her in my life again.

And with that one bleak thought, my world goes black.

Catherine and Charles's story continues in *The Enlightenment Series, Book 2, Enlighten You* by C.M. Swan.

www.ingramcontent.com/pod-product-compliance
Lightning Source LLC
Chambersburg PA
CBHW030547130626
46552CB00006B/2461